The Ballad of YaYa

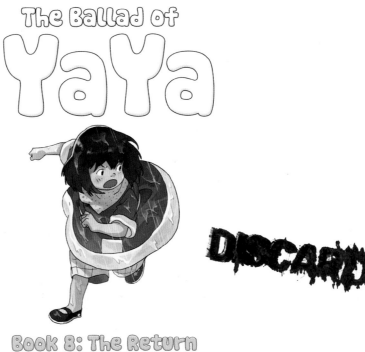

Book 8: The Return

Written by
Jean-Marie **Omont**

Illustrated by
Golo **Zhao**

Created and Edited by
Patrick **Marty** and Charlotte **Girard**

Translation and Layout by Mike Kennedy

MAGNETIC™

www.magnetic-press.com

YAYA AND ZHU HAVE BOARDED A SHIP HEADING BACK TO SHANGHAI, WHERE THEY HOPE TO FINALLY FIND HER PARENTS. BUT BECAUSE OF YAYA'S AMNESIA, SHE STILL DOESN'T REALIZE THAT ZHU IS THE GANGSTER WHO HAS BEEN CHASING HER SINCE THE JAPANESE ATTACK ON THE HARBOR. HE JUST WANTS TO RANSOM HER BACK TO HER PARENTS FOR A BIG REWARD!

MEANWHILE, TUDUO AND OYSTER GRAVY RACE BACK TO SHANGHAI TOO WITH THE HOPE OF GETTING THERE BEFORE ZHU CAN EXECUTE HIS WICKED PLAN!

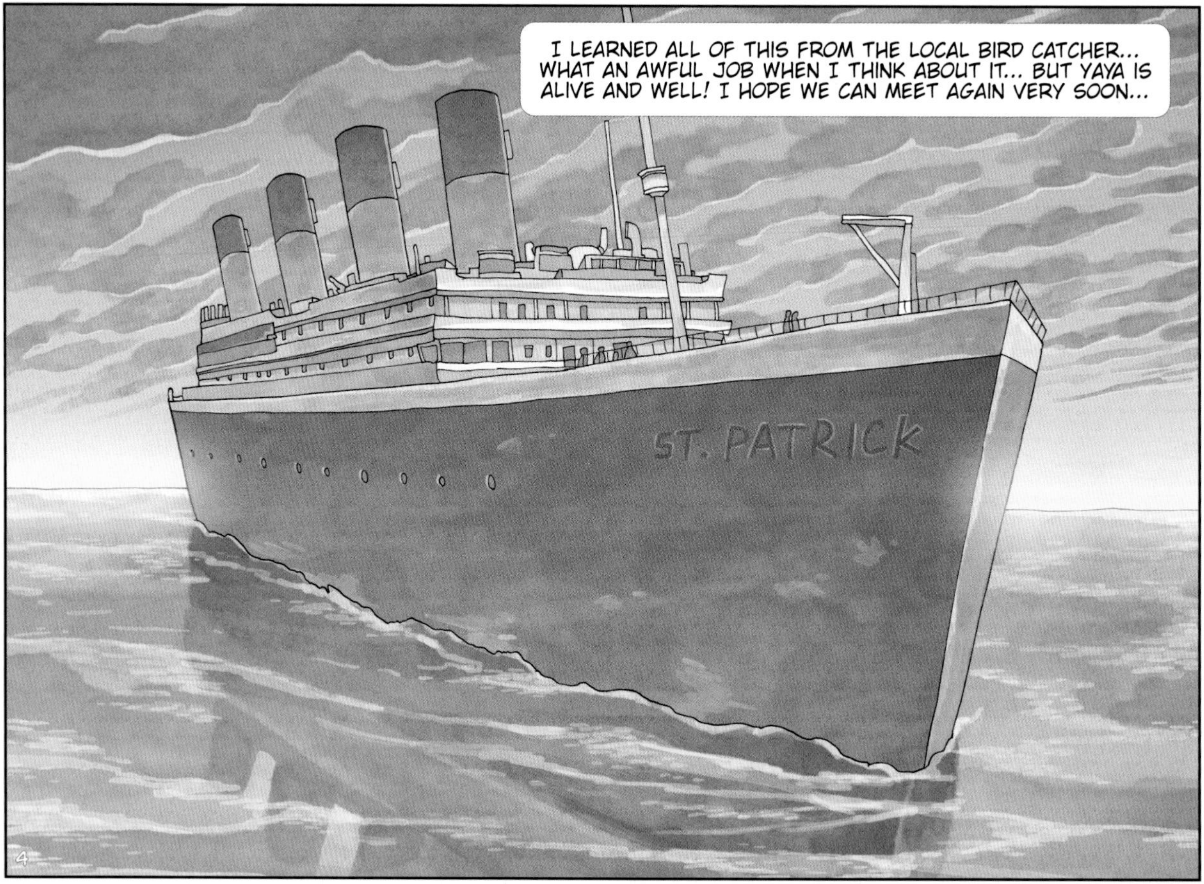
I LEARNED ALL OF THIS FROM THE LOCAL BIRD CATCHER... WHAT AN AWFUL JOB WHEN I THINK ABOUT IT... BUT YAYA IS ALIVE AND WELL! I HOPE WE CAN MEET AGAIN VERY SOON...
ST. PATRICK

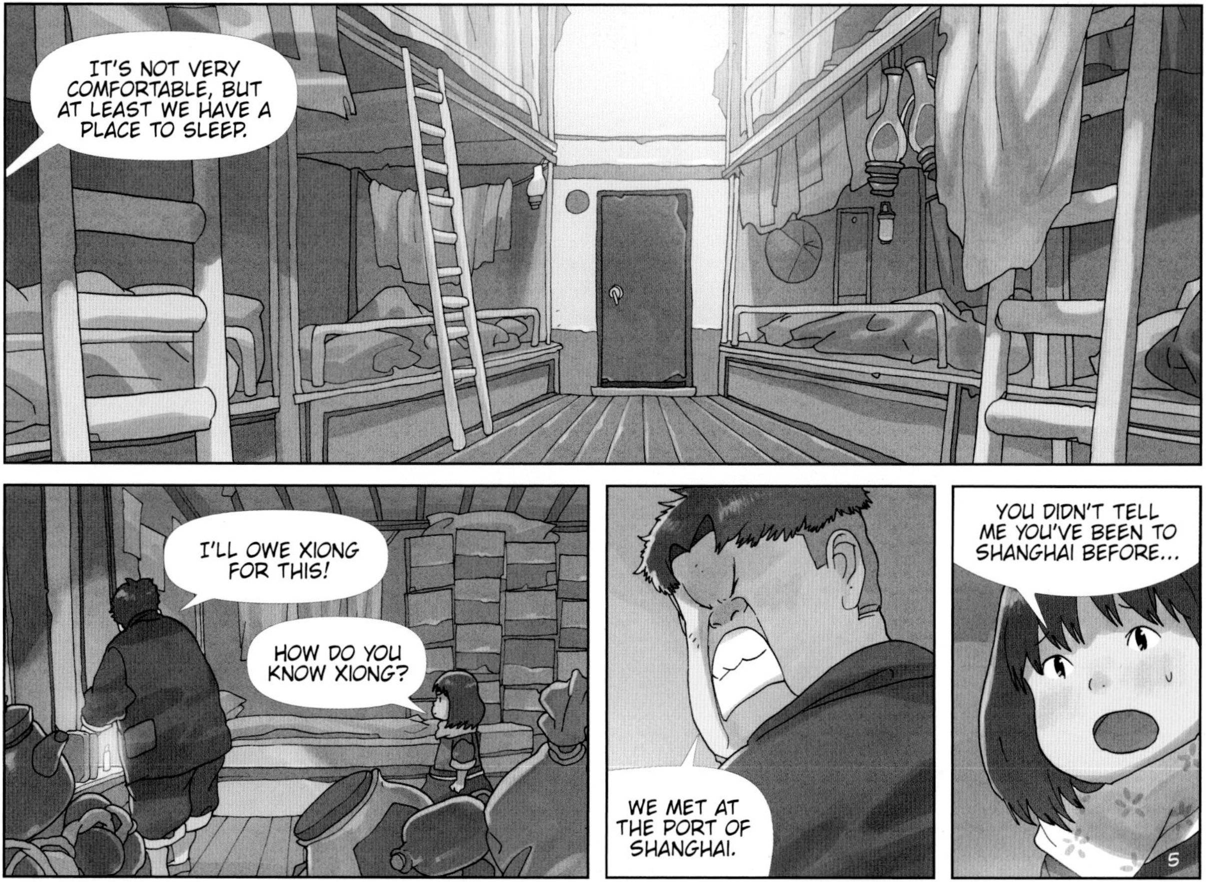
IT'S NOT VERY COMFORTABLE, BUT AT LEAST WE HAVE A PLACE TO SLEEP.
I'LL OWE XIONG FOR THIS!
HOW DO YOU KNOW XIONG?
WE MET AT THE PORT OF SHANGHAI.
YOU DIDN'T TELL ME YOU'VE BEEN TO SHANGHAI BEFORE...
5

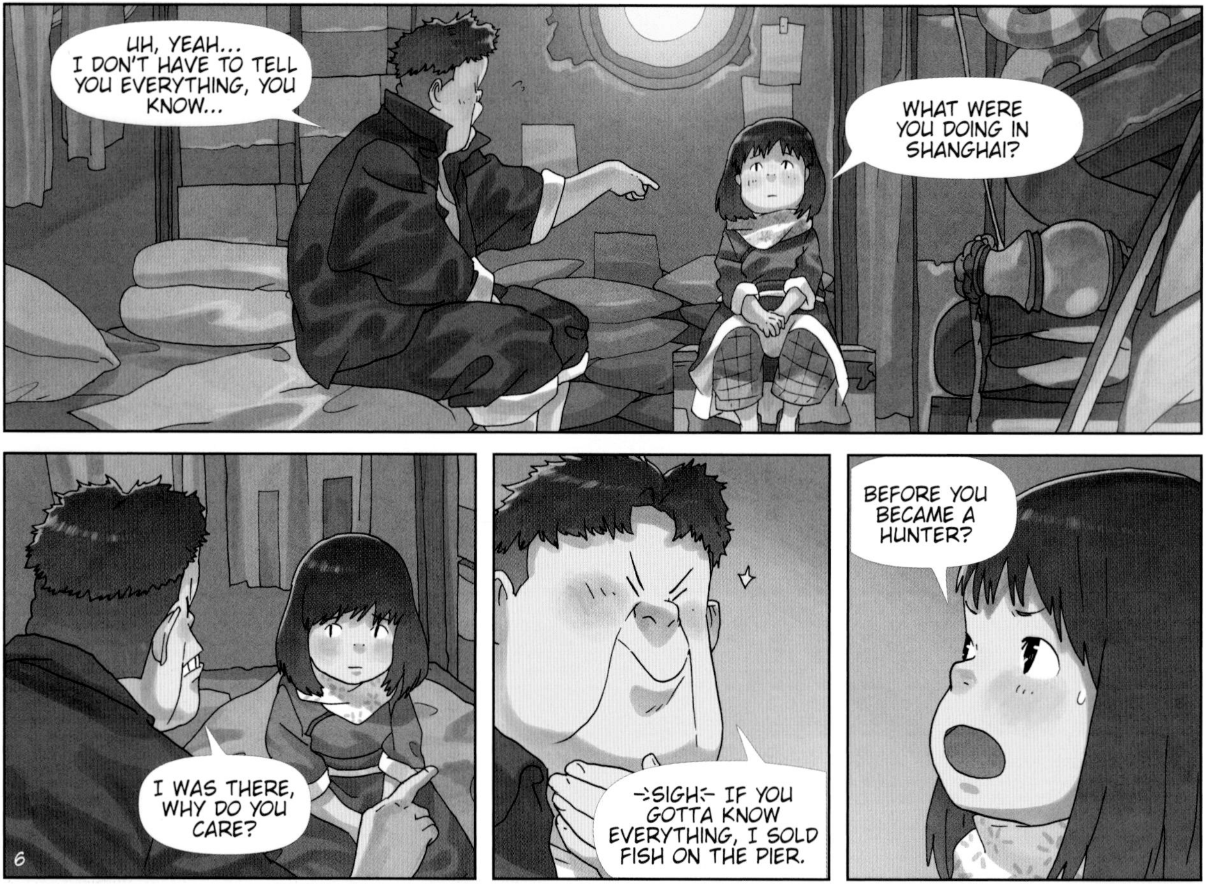

UH, YEAH...
I DON'T HAVE TO TELL YOU EVERYTHING, YOU KNOW...
WHAT WERE YOU DOING IN SHANGHAI?
I WAS THERE, WHY DO YOU CARE?
-SIGH- IF YOU GOTTA KNOW EVERYTHING, I SOLD FISH ON THE PIER.
BEFORE YOU BECAME A HUNTER?

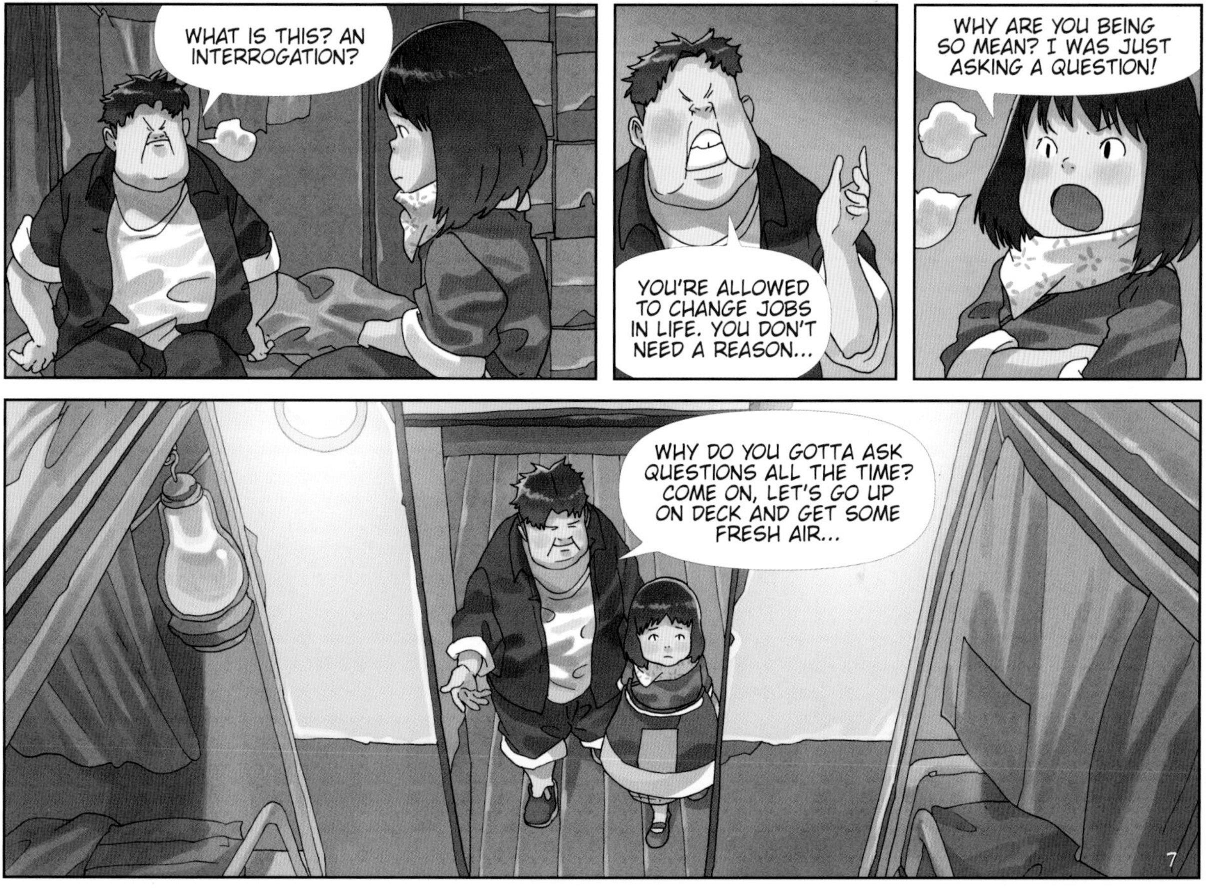
WHAT IS THIS? AN INTERROGATION?
YOU'RE ALLOWED TO CHANGE JOBS IN LIFE. YOU DON'T NEED A REASON...
WHY ARE YOU BEING SO MEAN? I WAS JUST ASKING A QUESTION!
WHY DO YOU GOTTA ASK QUESTIONS ALL THE TIME? COME ON, LET'S GO UP ON DECK AND GET SOME FRESH AIR...

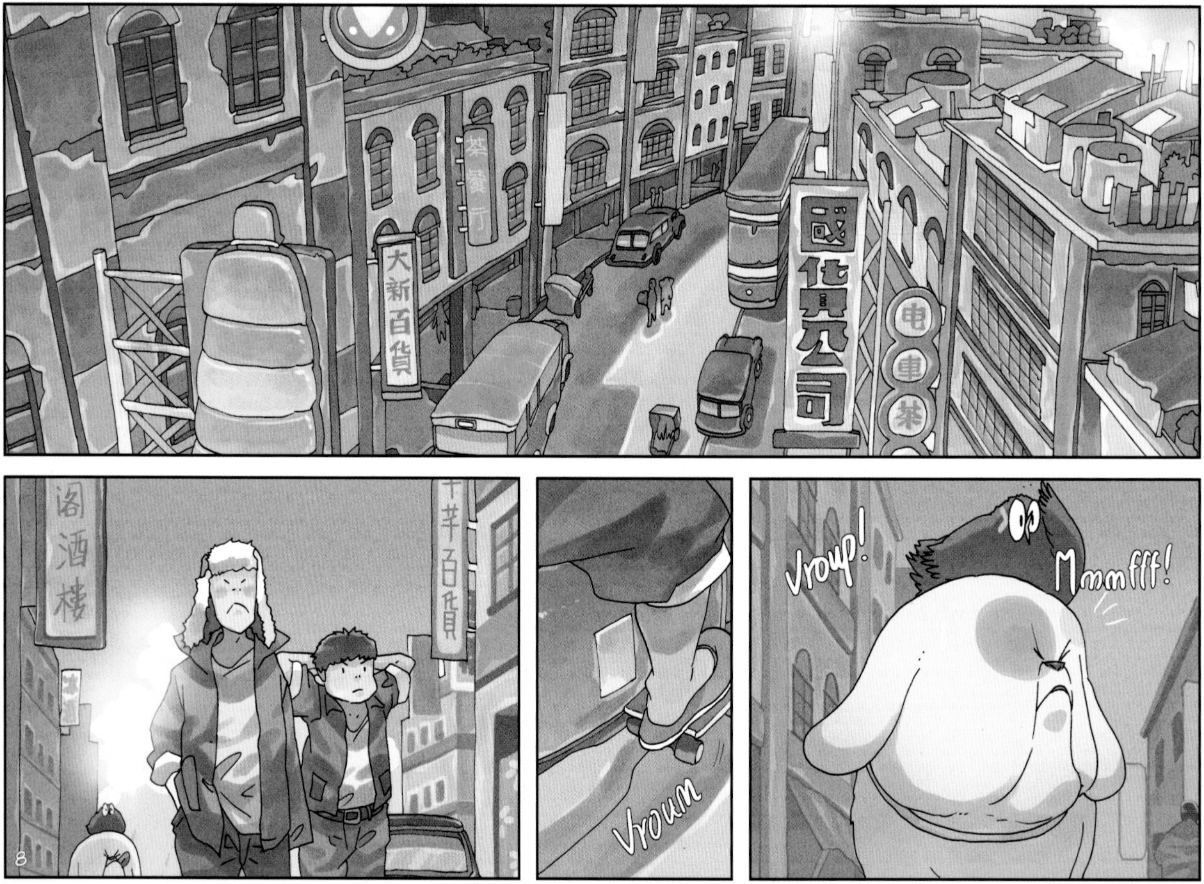
大新百貨
电
車
茶
Vroum
Vroup!
Mmmfff!

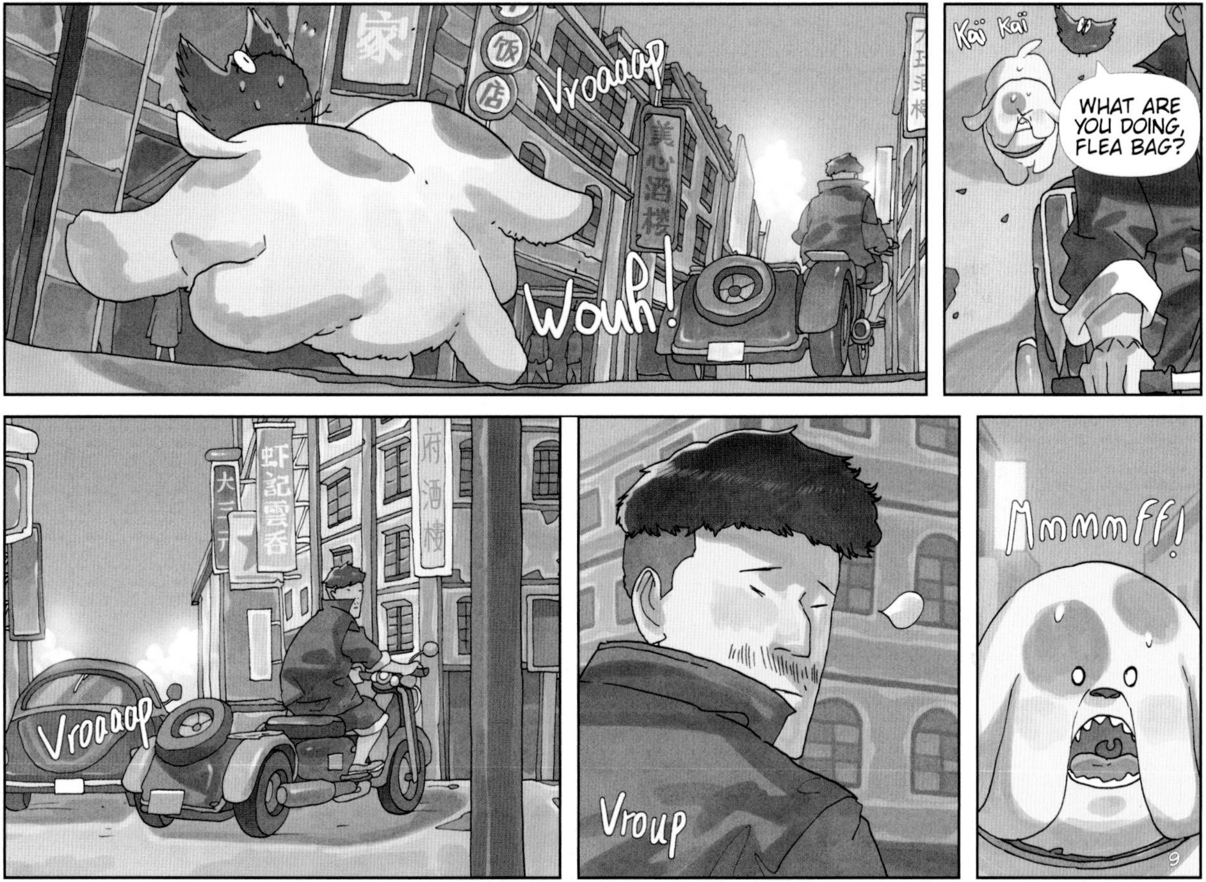
Vroaaap
Wouh!
Kaï Kaï
WHAT ARE YOU DOING, FLEA BAG?
Vroaaap
Vroup
Mmmmff!

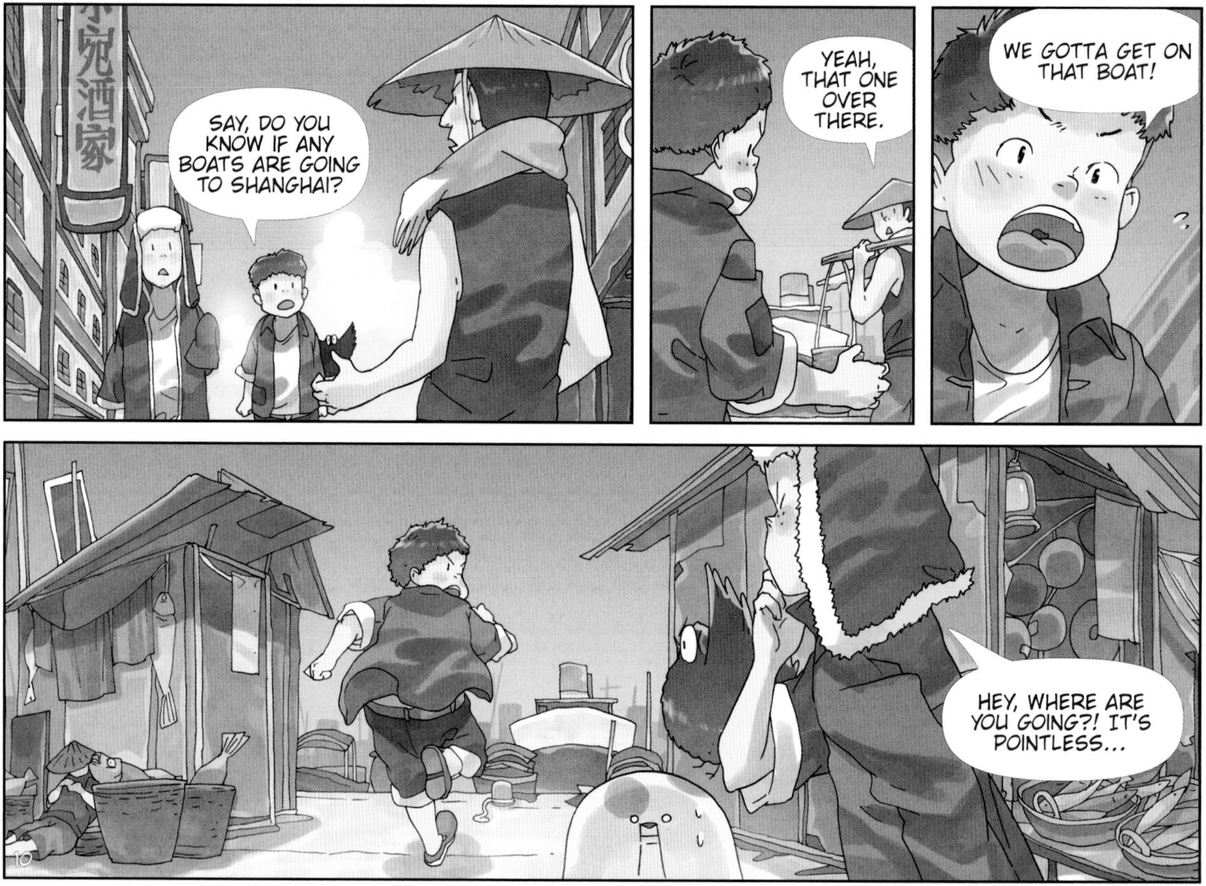
SAY, DO YOU KNOW IF ANY BOATS ARE GOING TO SHANGHAI?
YEAH, THAT ONE OVER THERE.
WE GOTTA GET ON THAT BOAT!
HEY, WHERE ARE YOU GOING?! IT'S POINTLESS...

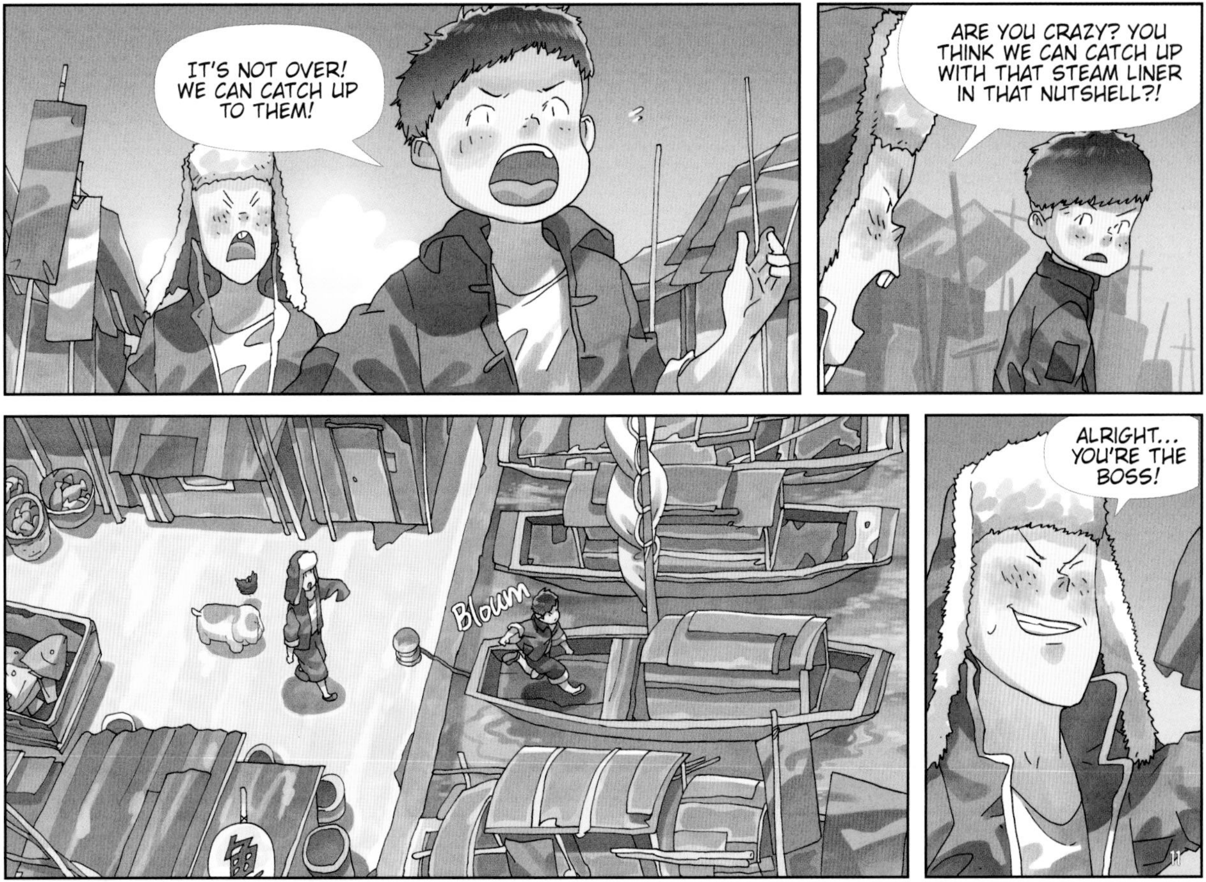
IT'S NOT OVER! WE CAN CATCH UP TO THEM!
ARE YOU CRAZY? YOU THINK WE CAN CATCH UP WITH THAT STEAM LINER IN THAT NUTSHELL?!
Bloum
ALRIGHT... YOU'RE THE BOSS!

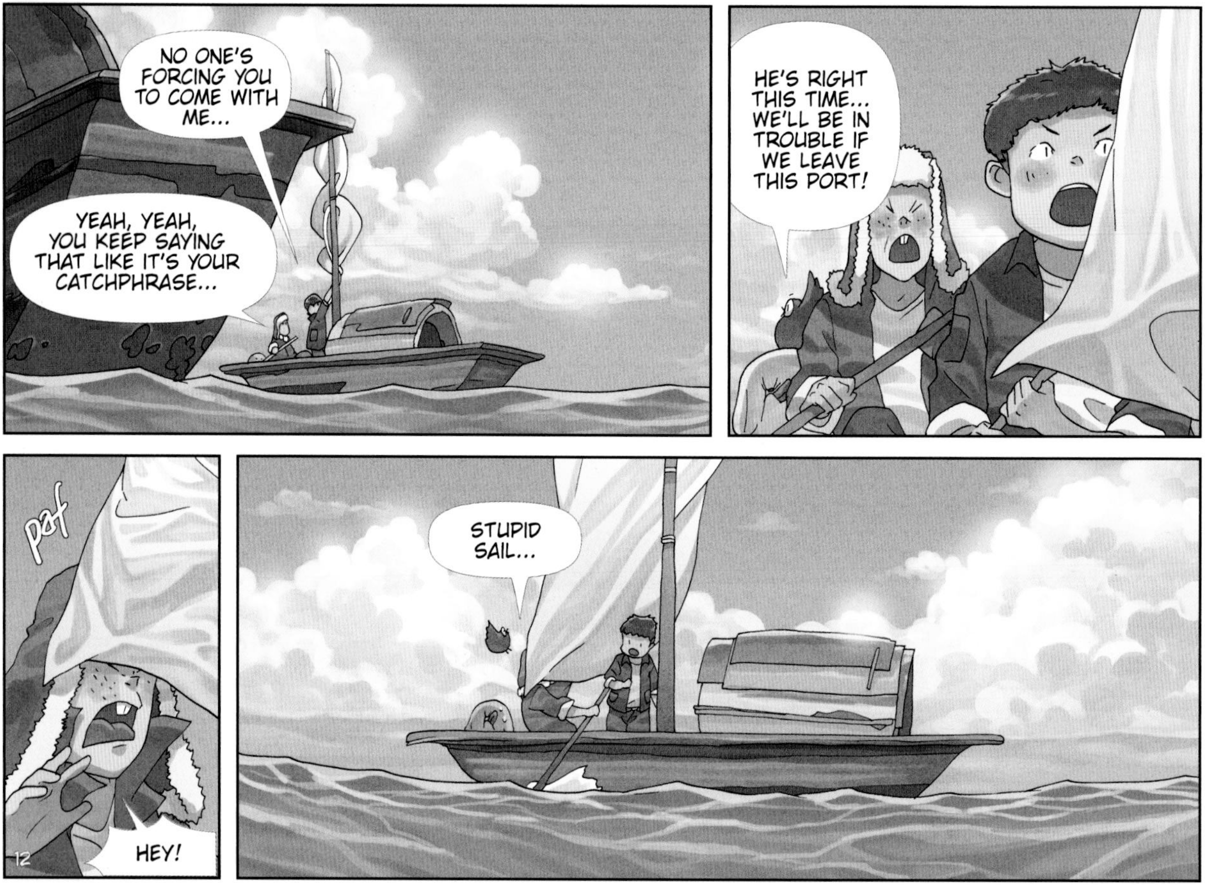
NO ONE'S FORCING YOU TO COME WITH ME...
YEAH, YEAH, YOU KEEP SAYING THAT LIKE IT'S YOUR CATCHPHRASE...
HE'S RIGHT THIS TIME... WE'LL BE IN TROUBLE IF WE LEAVE THIS PORT!
paf
HEY!
STUPID SAIL...

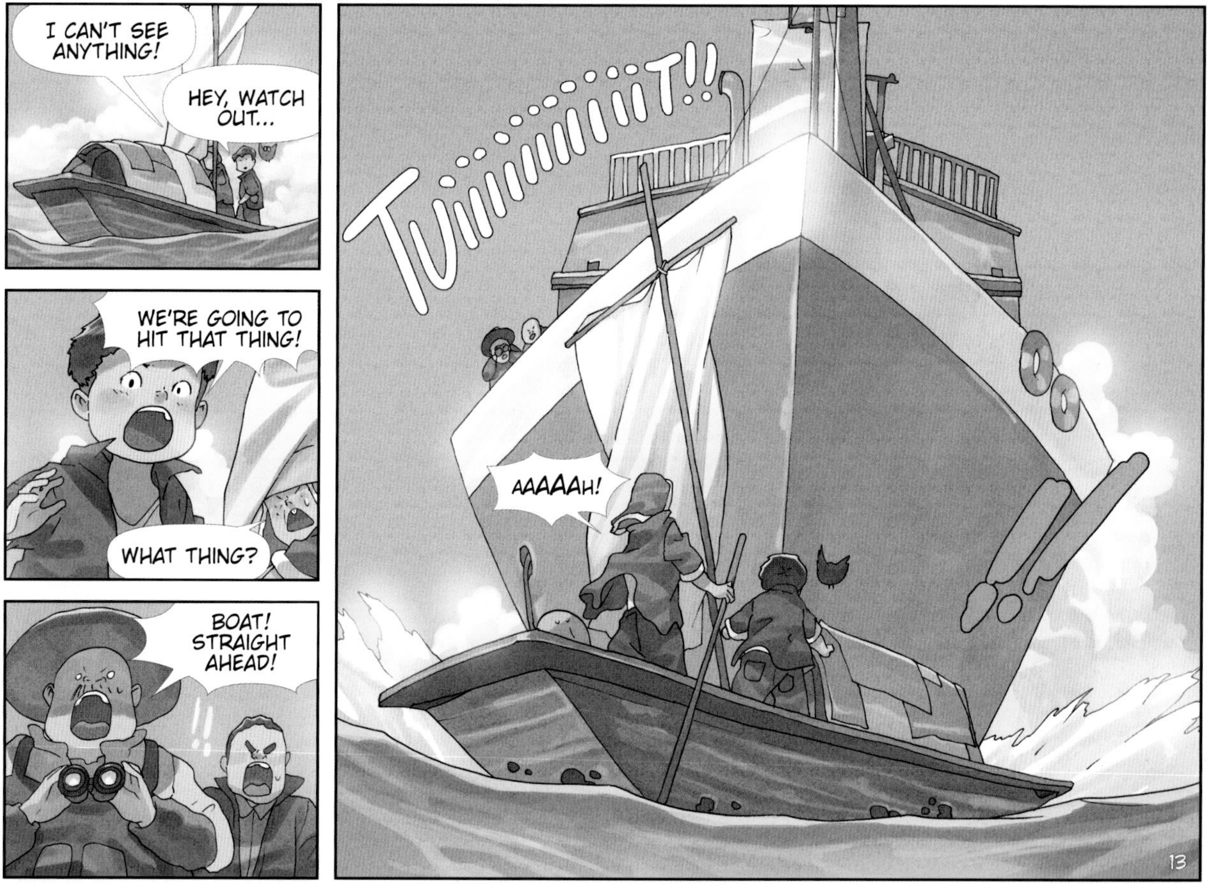
I CAN'T SEE ANYTHING!
HEY, WATCH OUT...
WE'RE GOING TO HIT THAT THING!
WHAT THING?
BOAT! STRAIGHT AHEAD!
!!
TUiiiiiiiiiiiiT!!
AAAAAH!

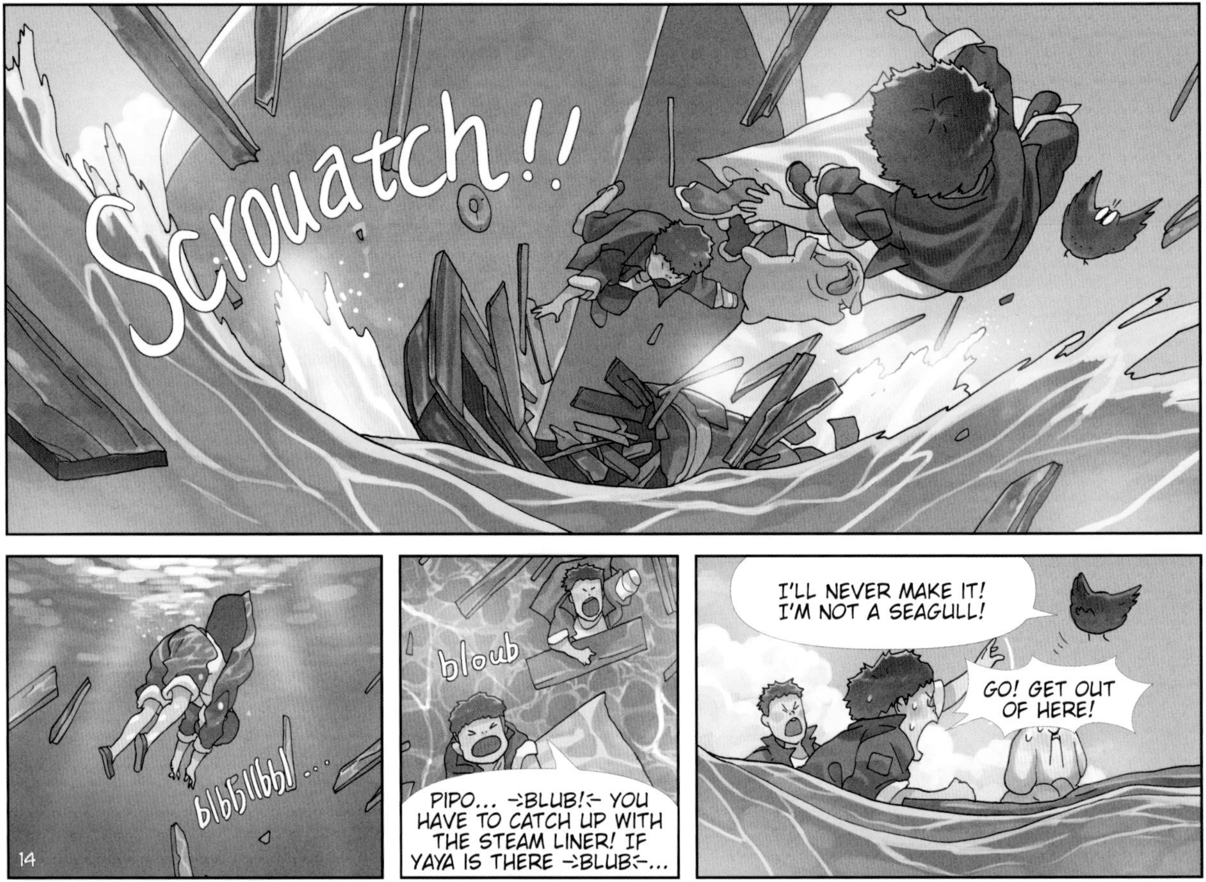
Scrouatch!!
blblllbbl...
bloub
PIPO... -BLUB!- YOU HAVE TO CATCH UP WITH THE STEAM LINER! IF YAYA IS THERE -BLUB-...
I'LL NEVER MAKE IT! I'M NOT A SEAGULL!
GO! GET OUT OF HERE!

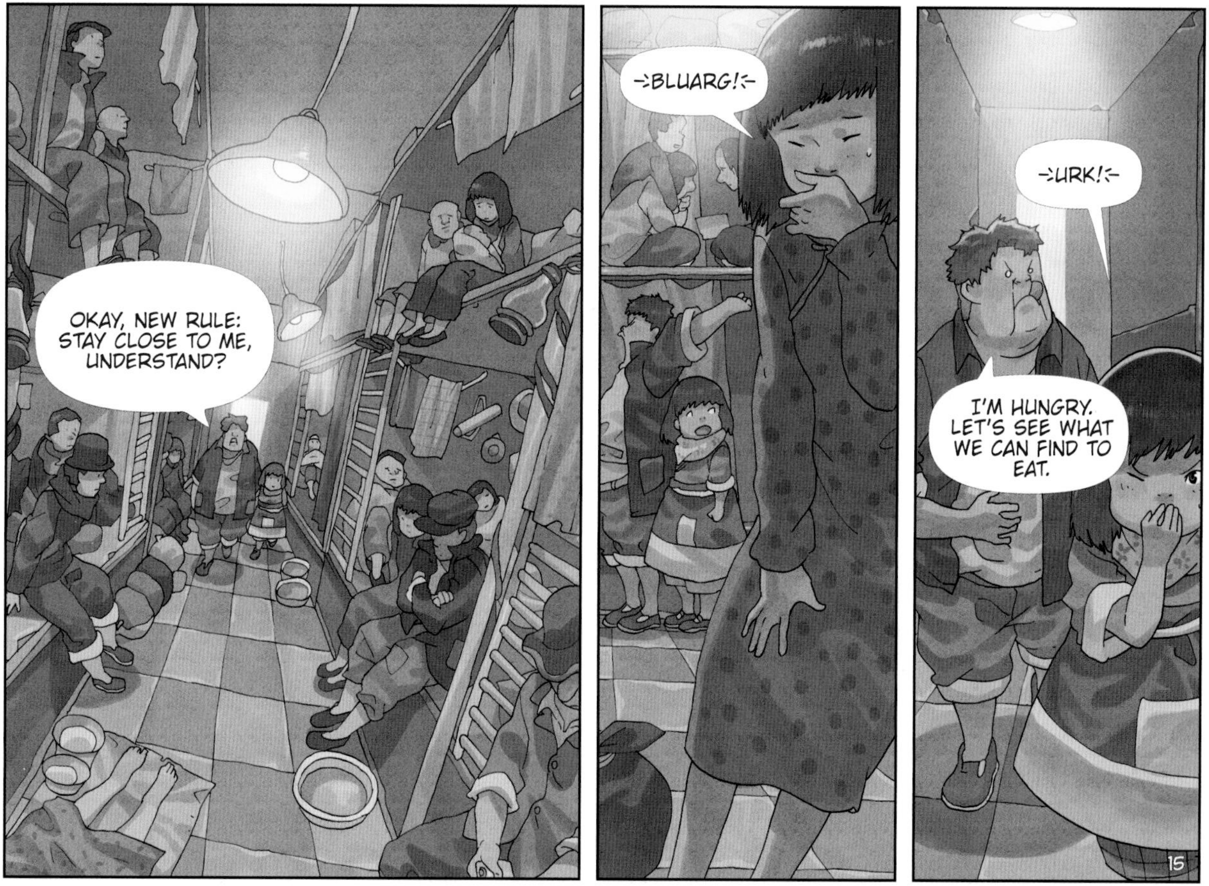
OKAY, NEW RULE: STAY CLOSE TO ME, UNDERSTAND?
-BLUARG!-
-URK!-
I'M HUNGRY. LET'S SEE WHAT WE CAN FIND TO EAT.

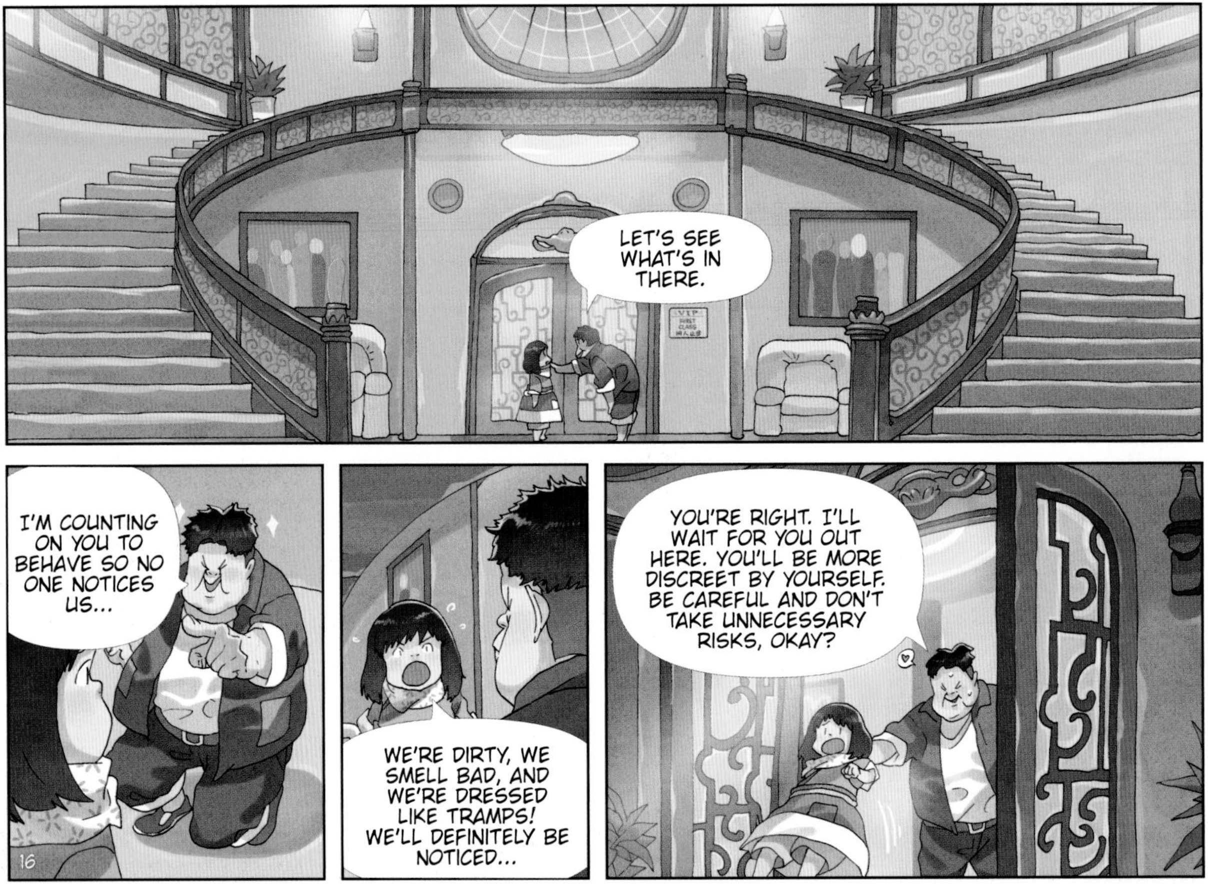
LET'S SEE WHAT'S IN THERE.
I'M COUNTING ON YOU TO BEHAVE SO NO ONE NOTICES US...
WE'RE DIRTY, WE SMELL BAD, AND WE'RE DRESSED LIKE TRAMPS! WE'LL DEFINITELY BE NOTICED...
YOU'RE RIGHT. I'LL WAIT FOR YOU OUT HERE. YOU'LL BE MORE DISCREET BY YOURSELF. BE CAREFUL AND DON'T TAKE UNNECESSARY RISKS, OKAY?

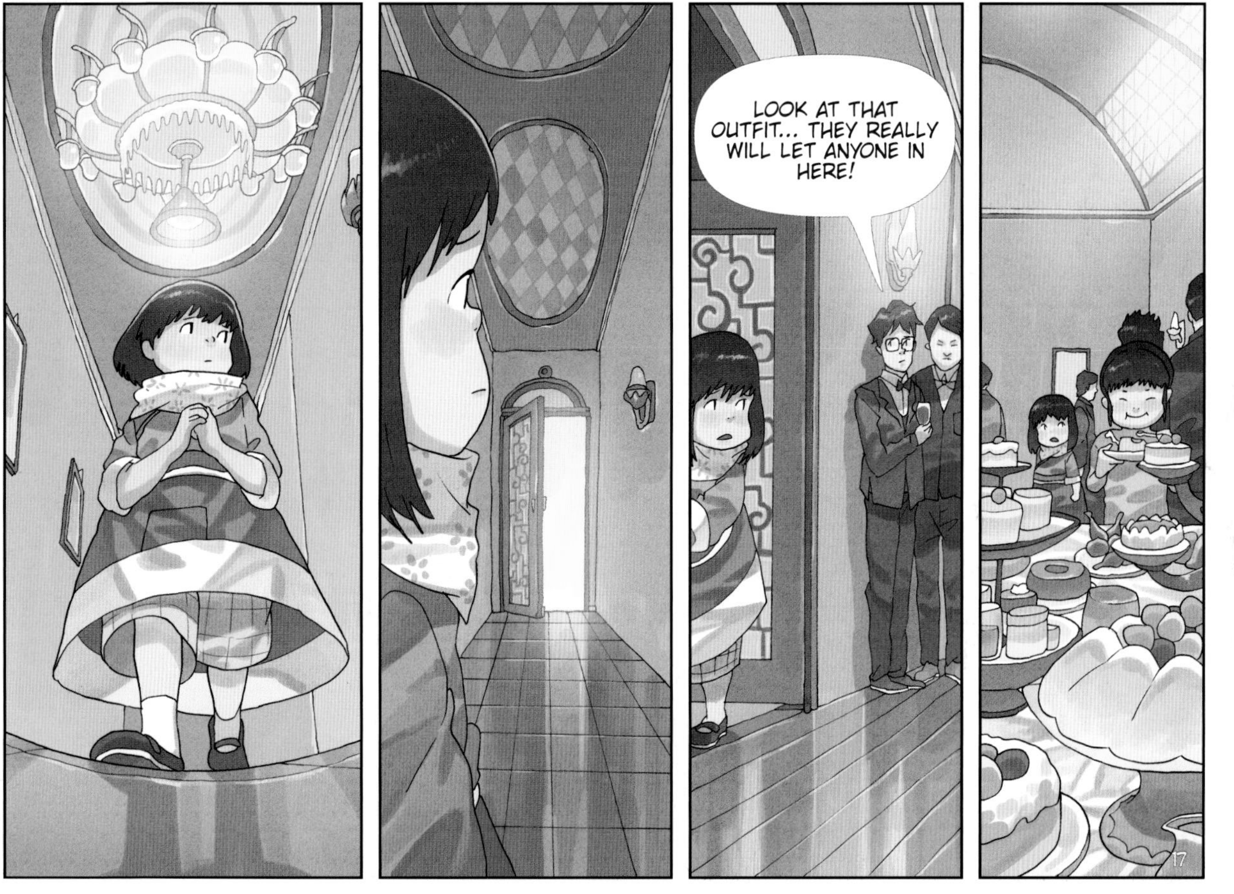
LOOK AT THAT OUTFIT... THEY REALLY WILL LET ANYONE IN HERE!

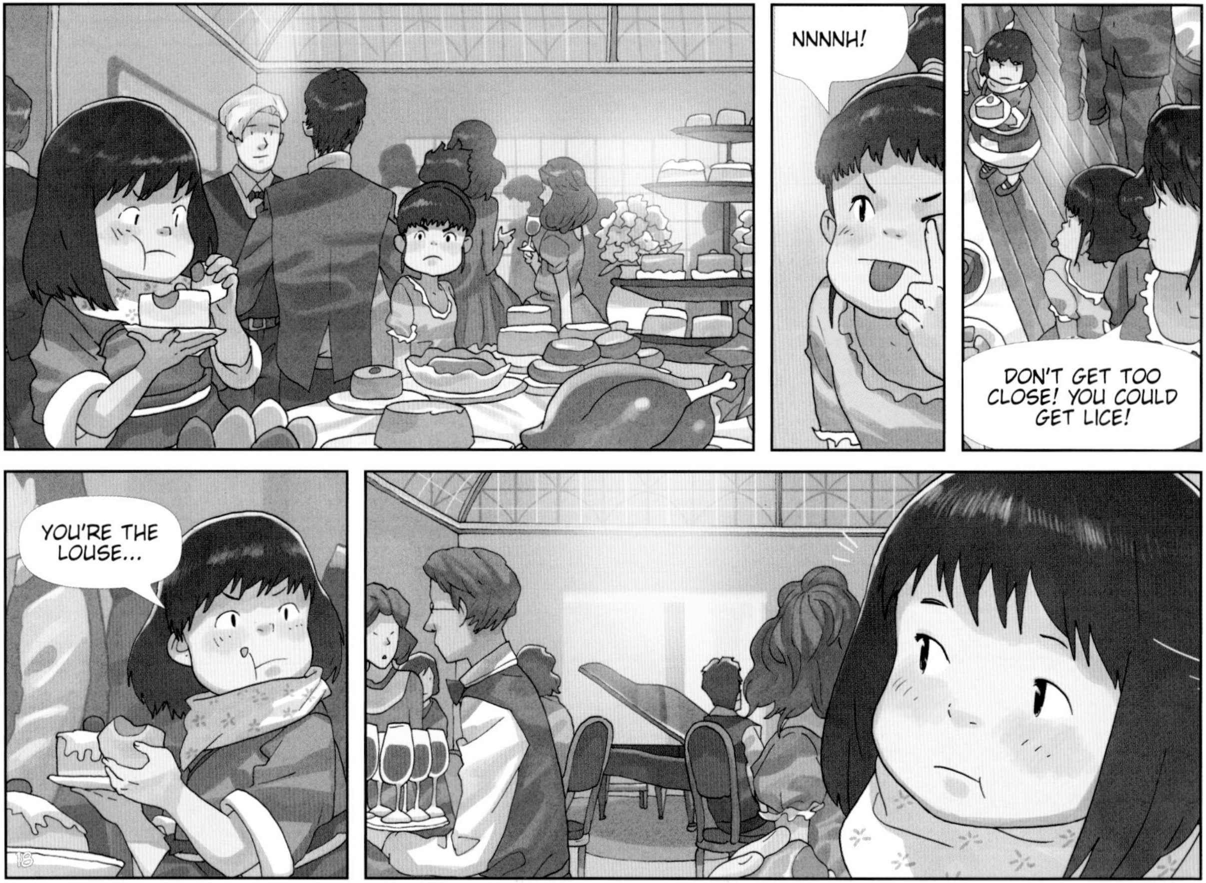

NNNNH!
DON'T GET TOO CLOSE! YOU COULD GET LICE!
YOU'RE THE LOUSE...

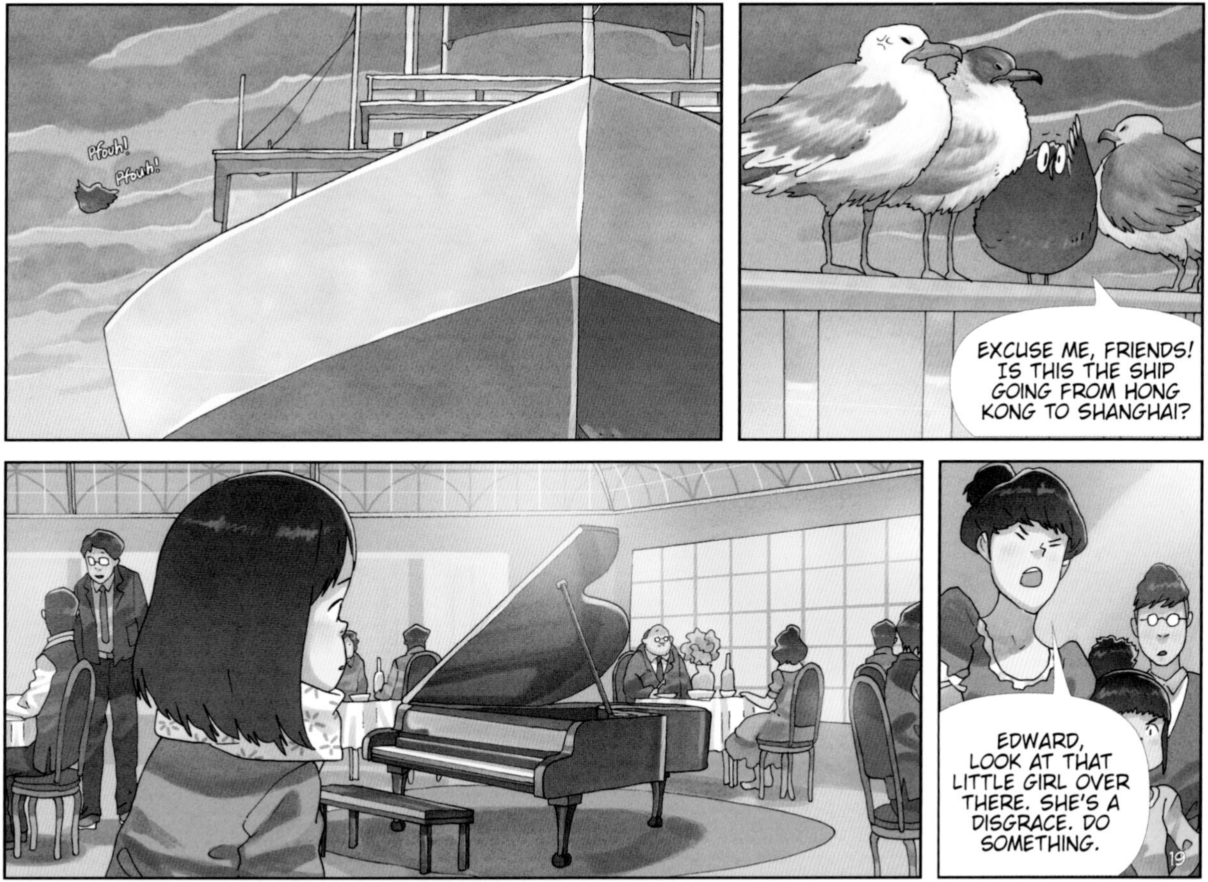
Pfouh!
Pfouh!
EXCUSE ME, FRIENDS! IS THIS THE SHIP GOING FROM HONG KONG TO SHANGHAI?
EDWARD, LOOK AT THAT LITTLE GIRL OVER THERE. SHE'S A DISGRACE. DO SOMETHING.

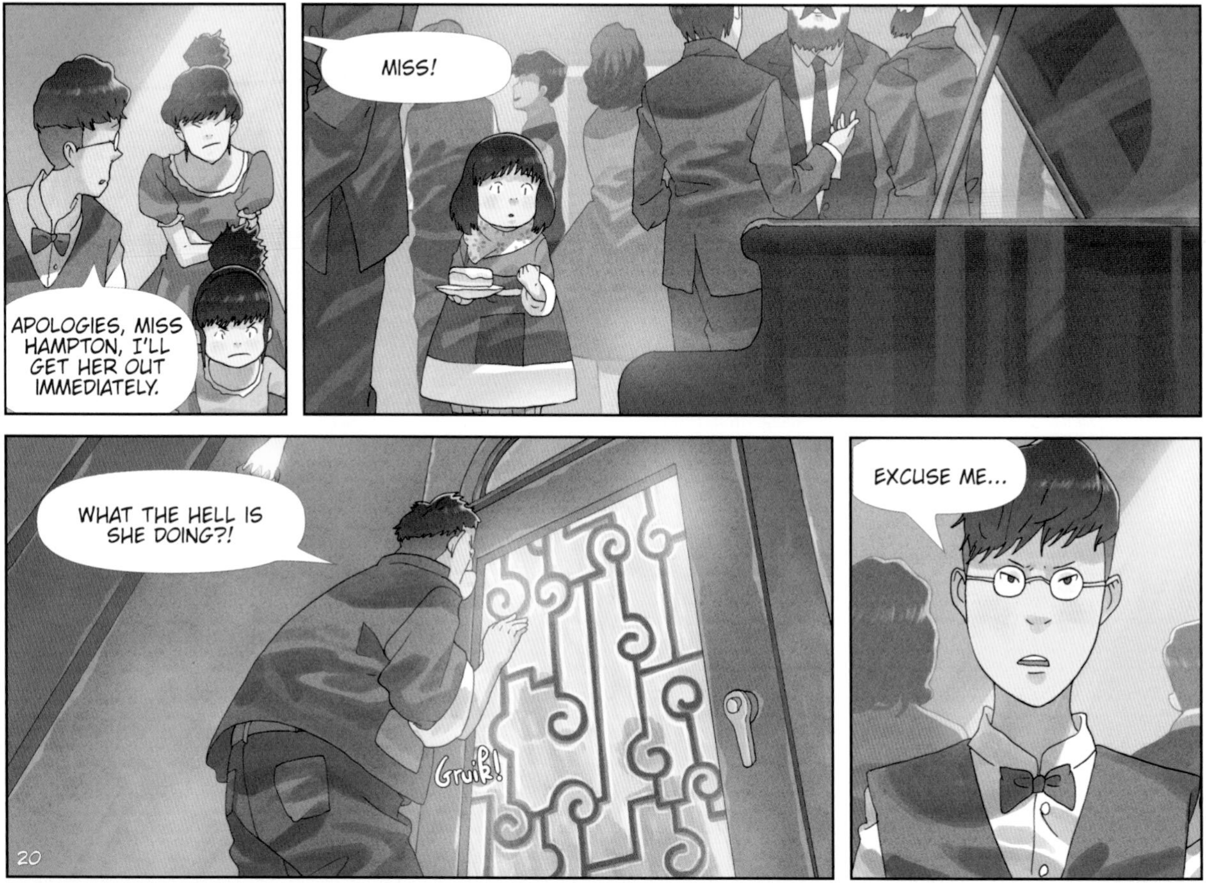
APOLOGIES, MISS HAMPTON, I'LL GET HER OUT IMMEDIATELY.
MISS!
WHAT THE HELL IS SHE DOING?!
Gruik!
EXCUSE ME...

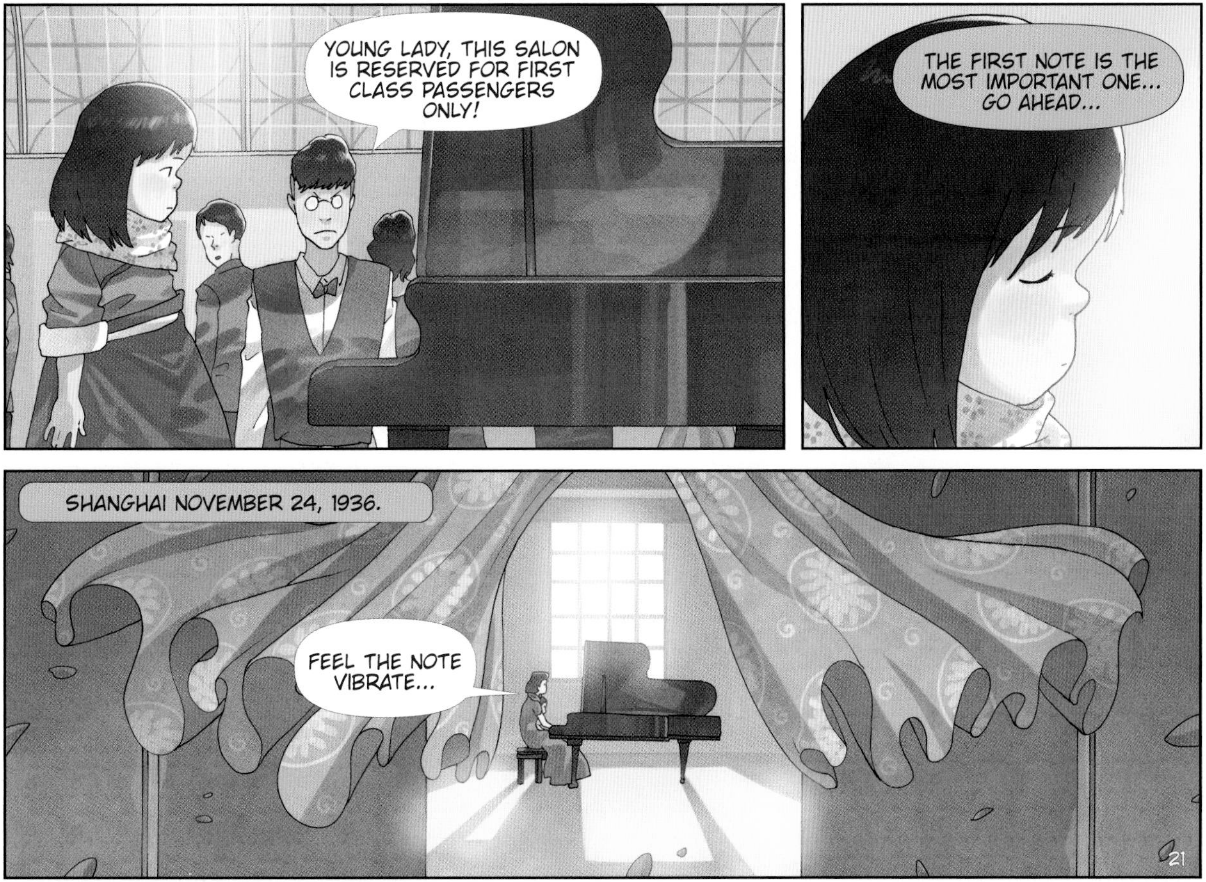
YOUNG LADY, THIS SALON IS RESERVED FOR FIRST CLASS PASSENGERS ONLY!
THE FIRST NOTE IS THE MOST IMPORTANT ONE... GO AHEAD...
SHANGHAI NOVEMBER 24, 1936.
FEEL THE NOTE VIBRATE...

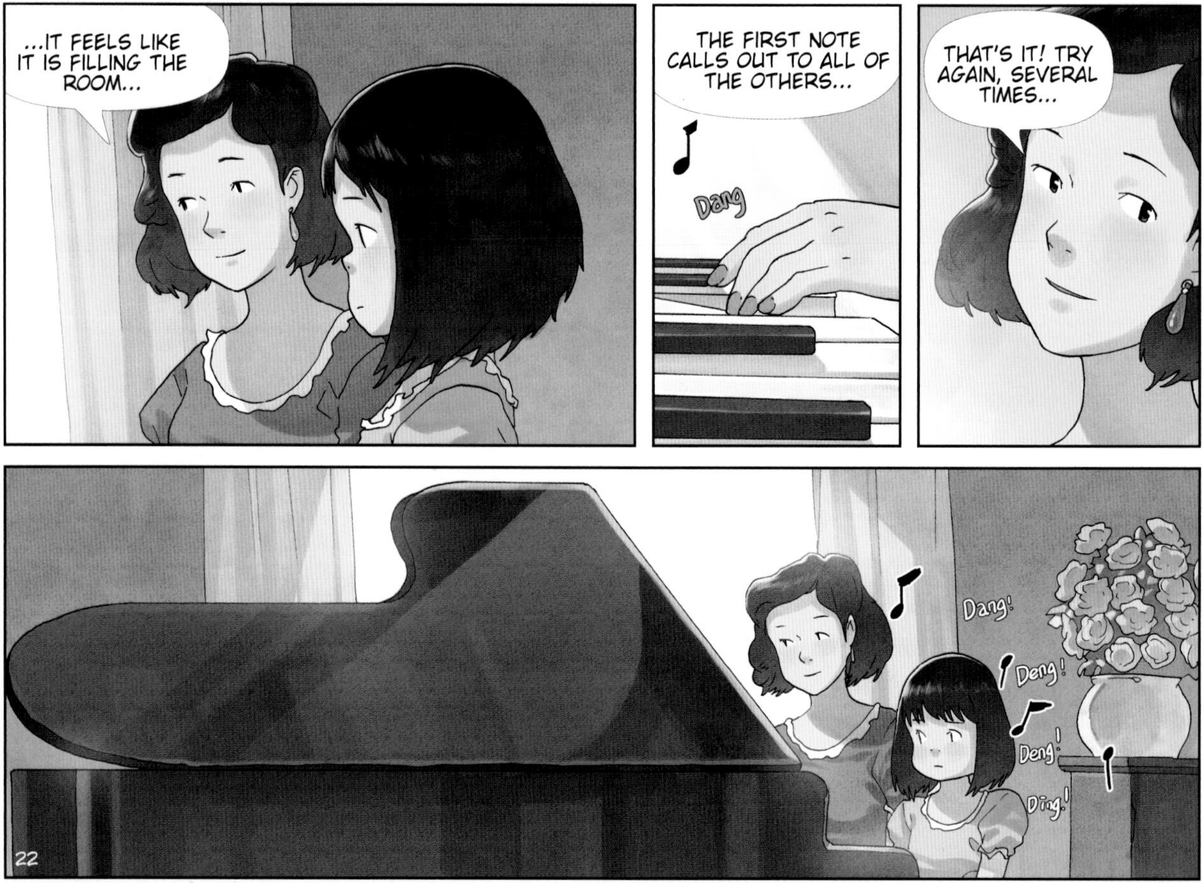
...IT FEELS LIKE IT IS FILLING THE ROOM...
THE FIRST NOTE CALLS OUT TO ALL OF THE OTHERS...
Dang
THAT'S IT! TRY AGAIN, SEVERAL TIMES...
Dang!
Deng!
Deng!
Ding!

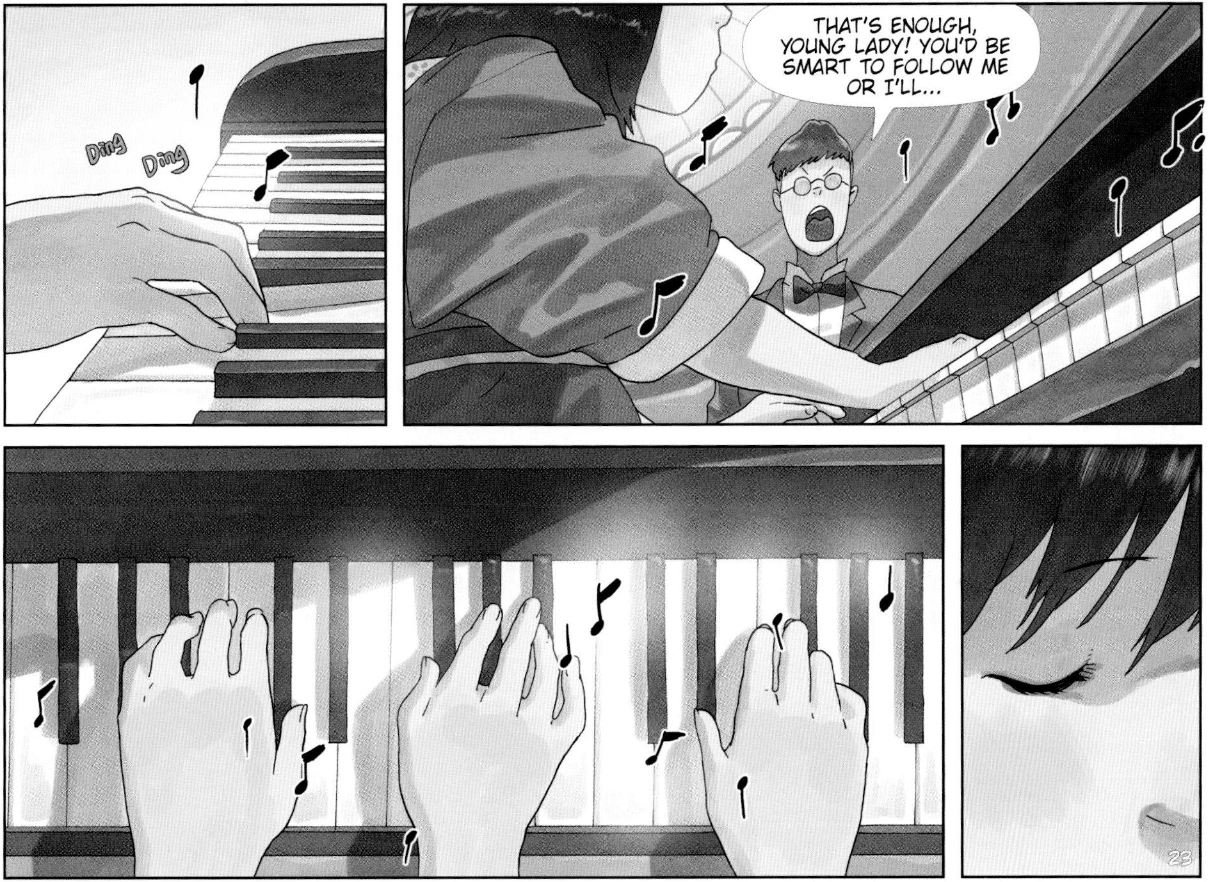
Ding
Ding
THAT'S ENOUGH, YOUNG LADY! YOU'D BE SMART TO FOLLOW ME OR I'LL...

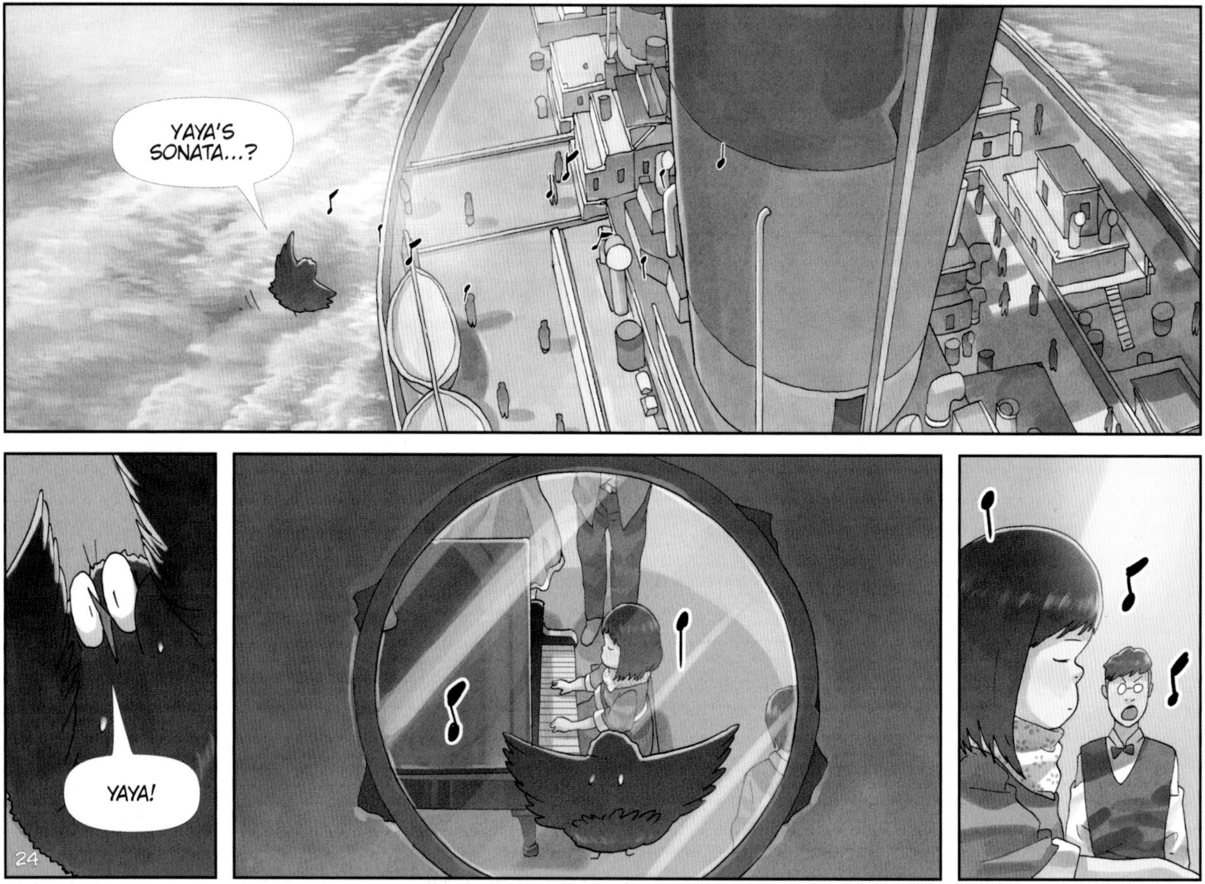
YAYA'S SONATA...?
YAYA!
24

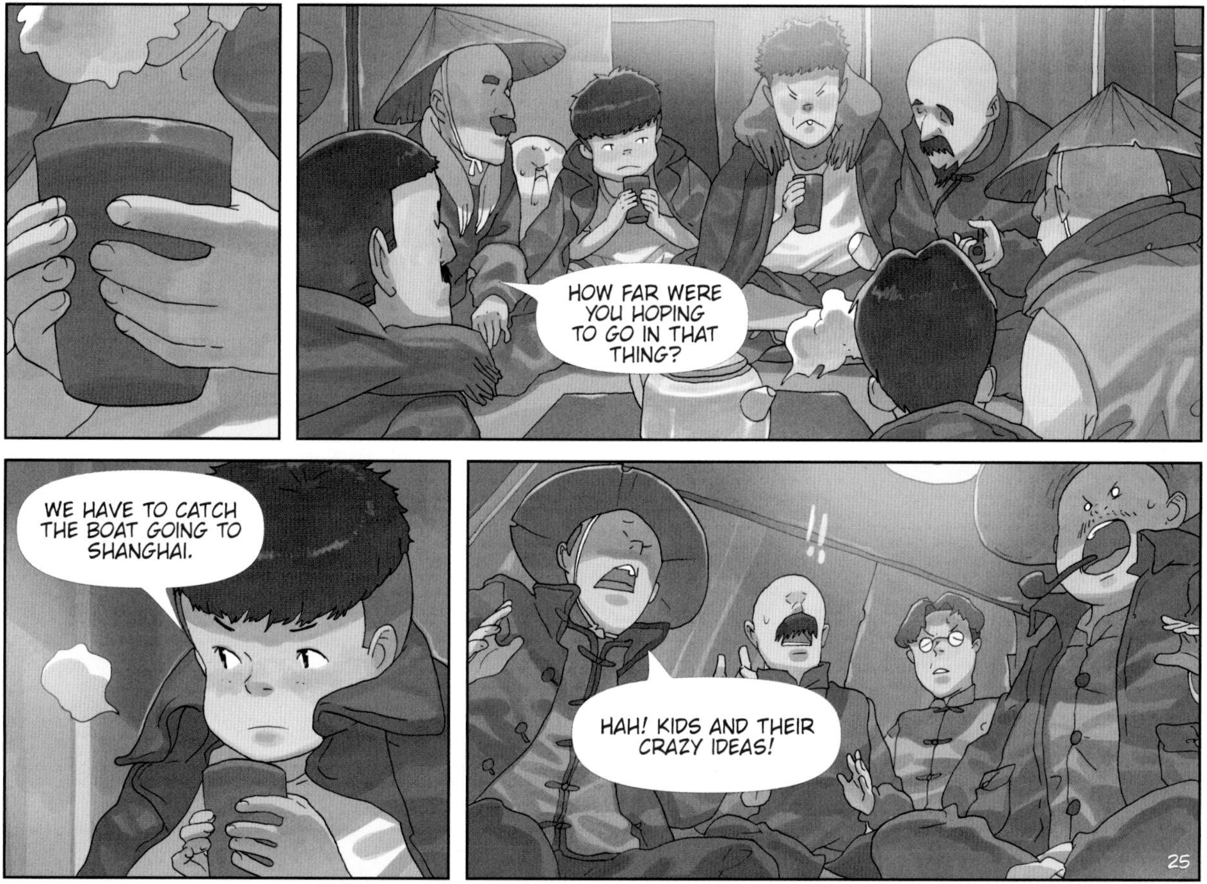
HOW FAR WERE YOU HOPING TO GO IN THAT THING?
WE HAVE TO CATCH THE BOAT GOING TO SHANGHAI.
!!
HAH! KIDS AND THEIR CRAZY IDEAS!

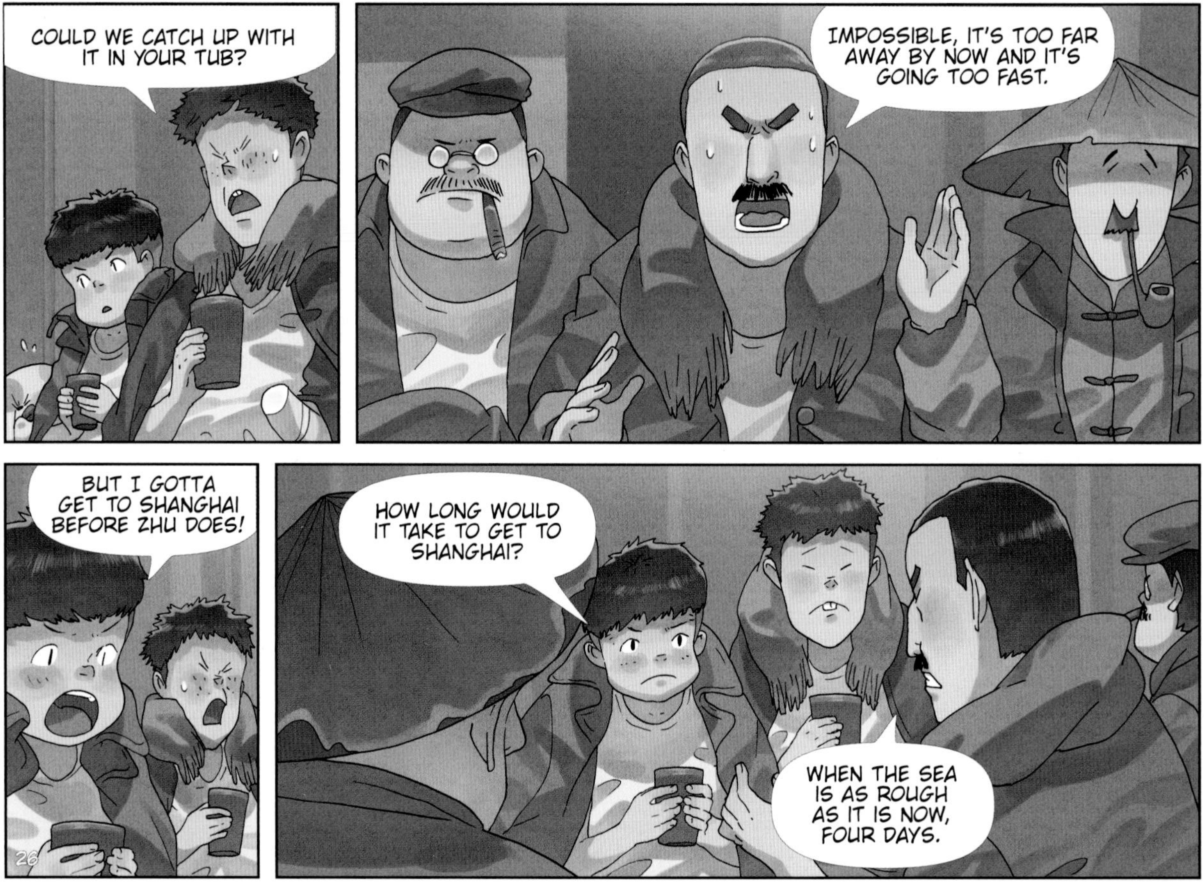
COULD WE CATCH UP WITH IT IN YOUR TUB?
IMPOSSIBLE, IT'S TOO FAR AWAY BY NOW AND IT'S GOING TOO FAST.
BUT I GOTTA GET TO SHANGHAI BEFORE ZHU DOES!
HOW LONG WOULD IT TAKE TO GET TO SHANGHAI?
WHEN THE SEA IS AS ROUGH AS IT IS NOW, FOUR DAYS.

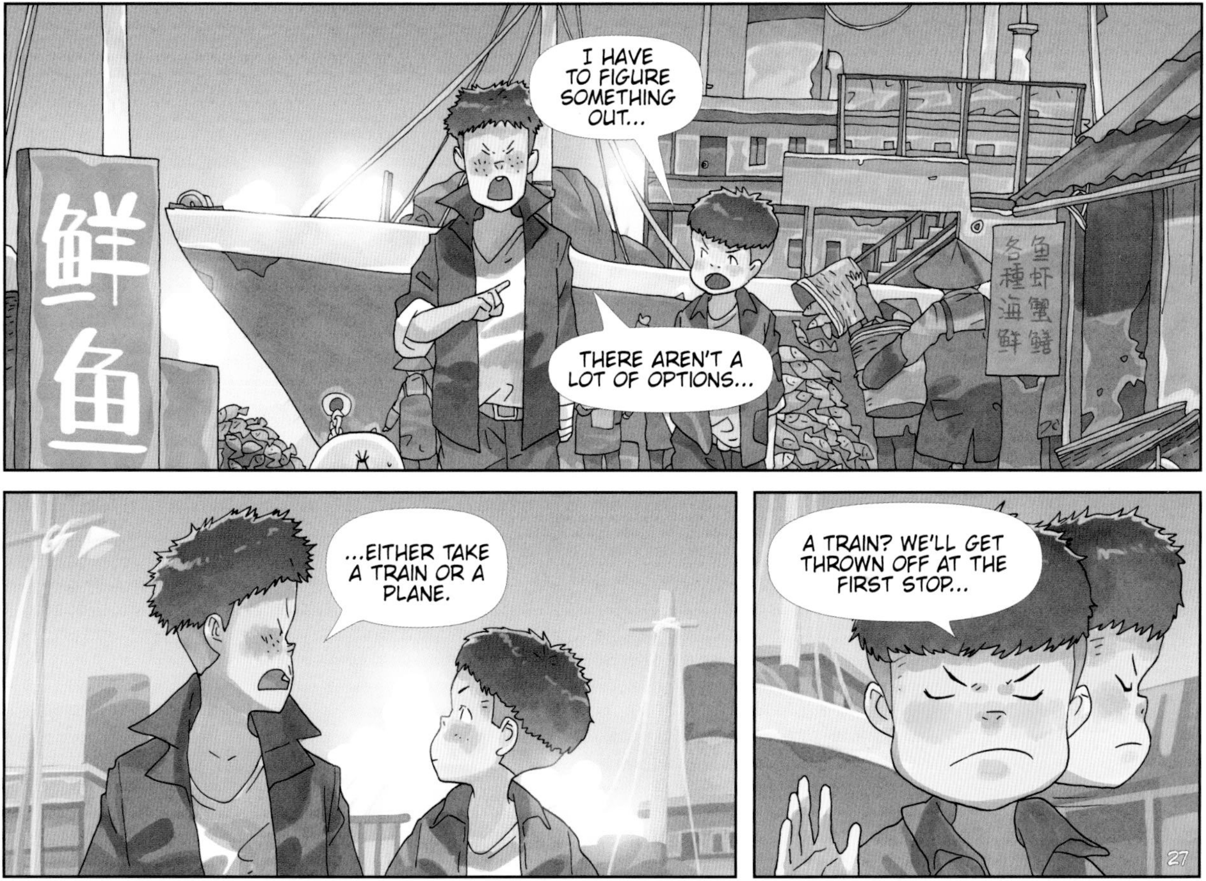
鲜鱼
I HAVE TO FIGURE SOMETHING OUT...
THERE AREN'T A LOT OF OPTIONS...
鱼虾蟹鳝
各種海鲜
...EITHER TAKE A TRAIN OR A PLANE.
A TRAIN? WE'LL GET THROWN OFF AT THE FIRST STOP...

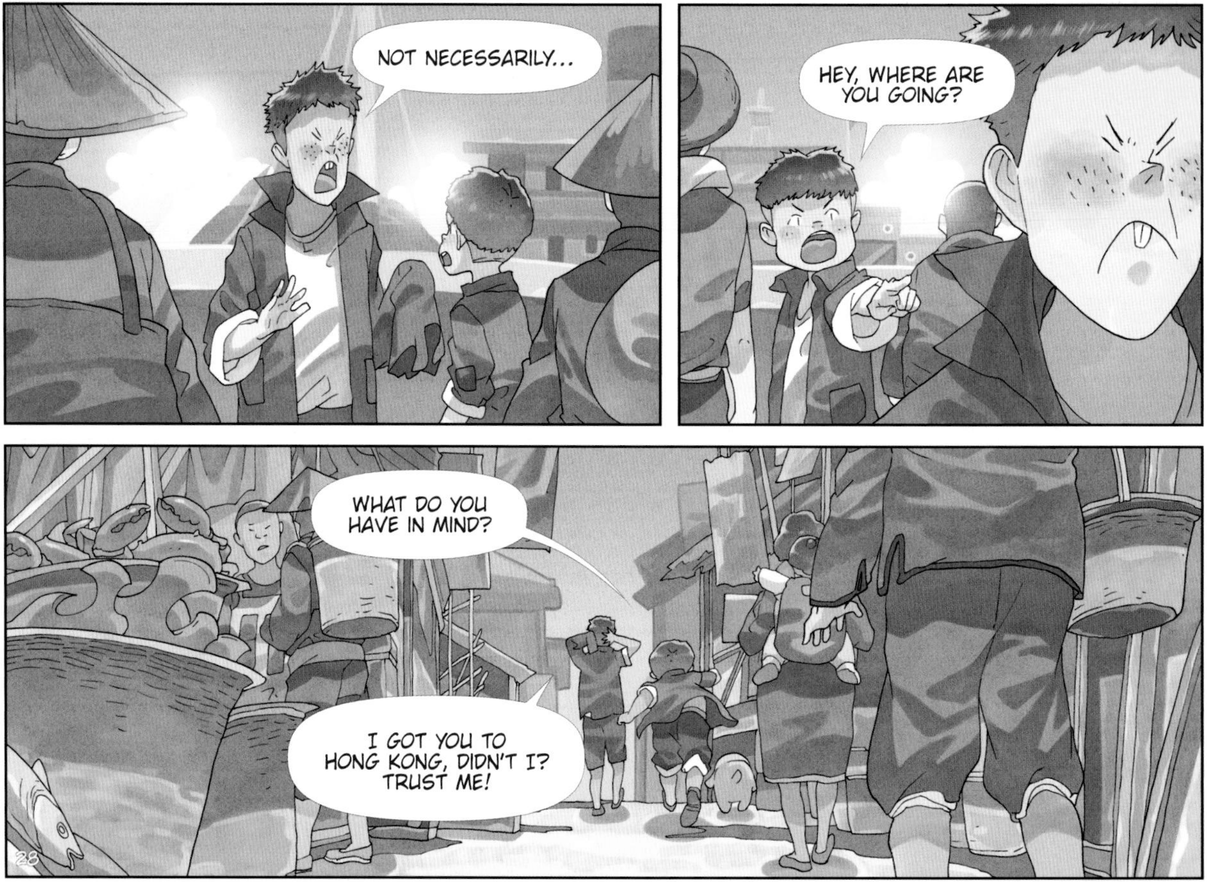
NOT NECESSARILY...
HEY, WHERE ARE YOU GOING?
WHAT DO YOU HAVE IN MIND?
I GOT YOU TO HONG KONG, DIDN'T I? TRUST ME!

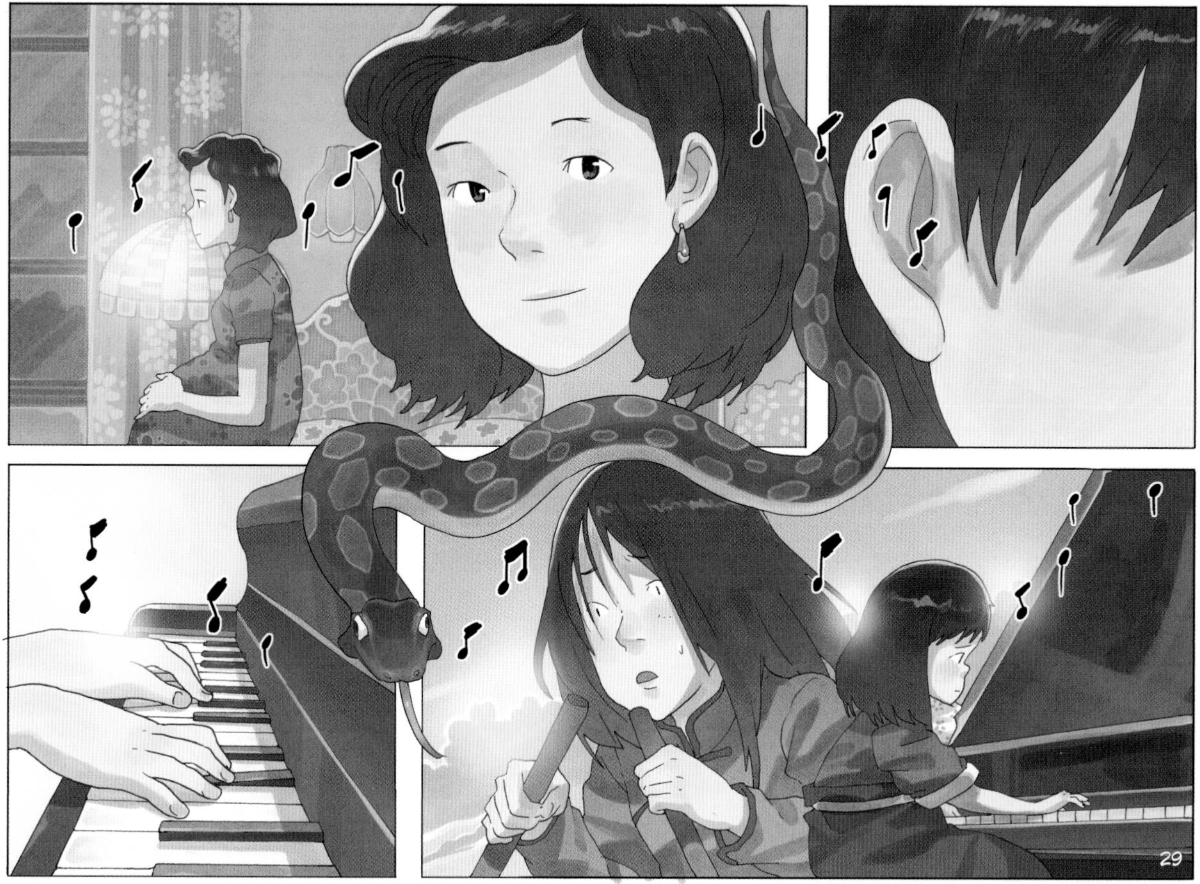

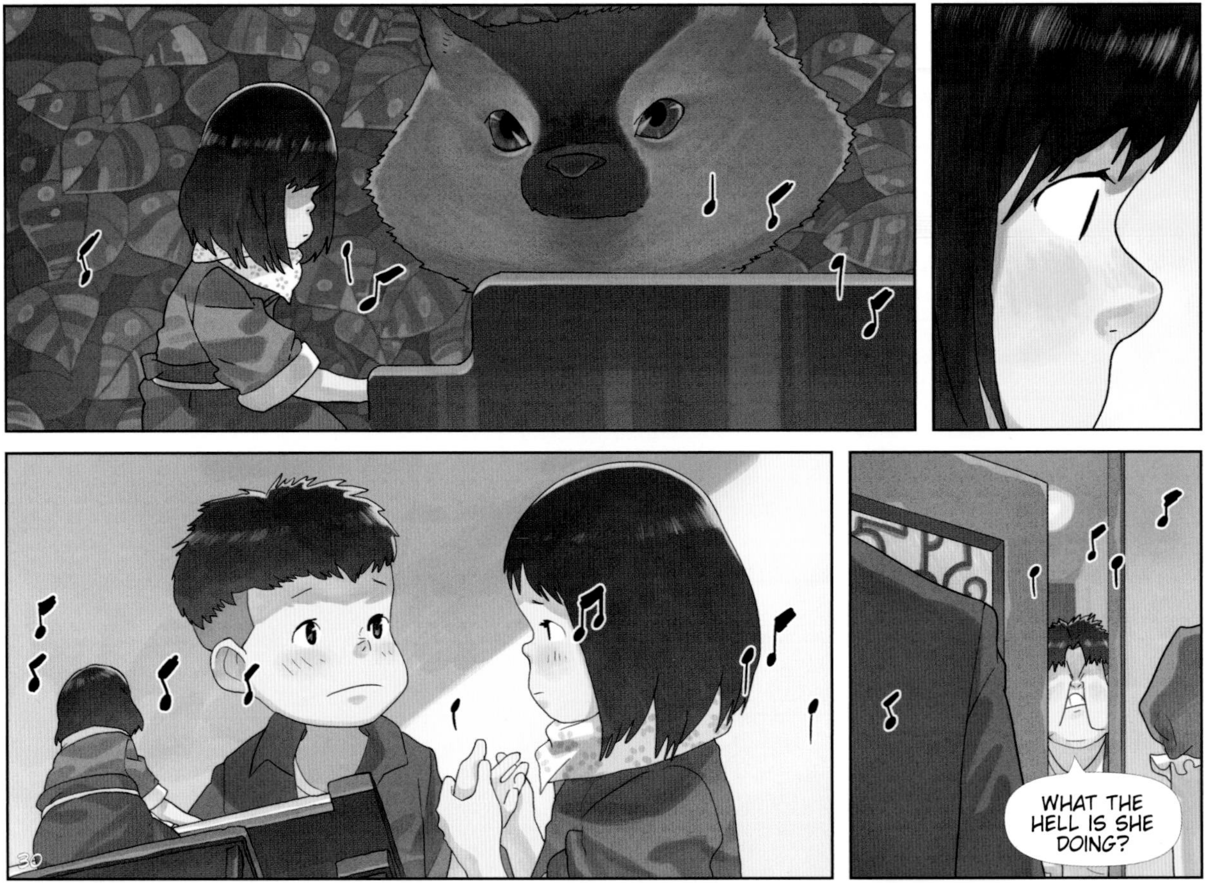
WHAT THE HELL IS SHE DOING?

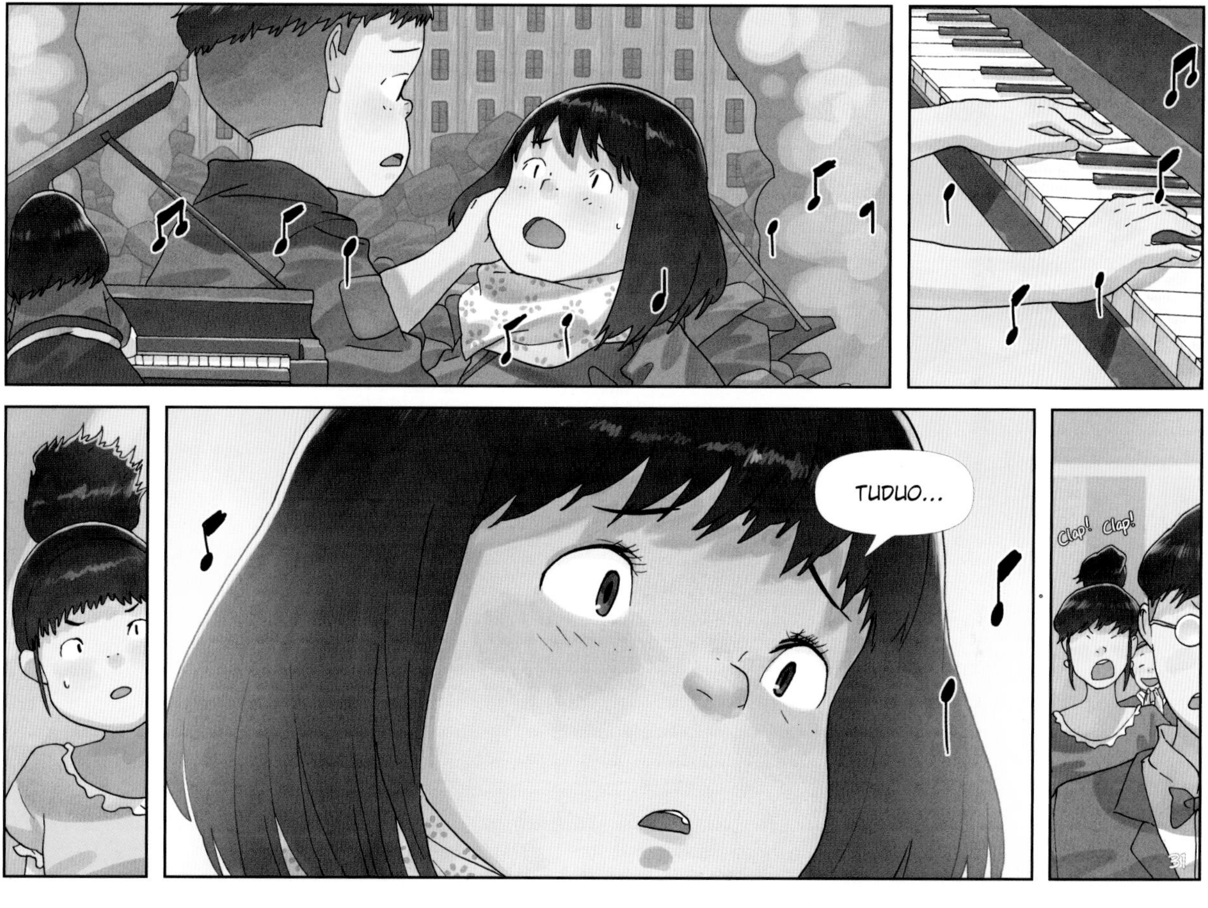
TUDUO...
Clap! Clap!

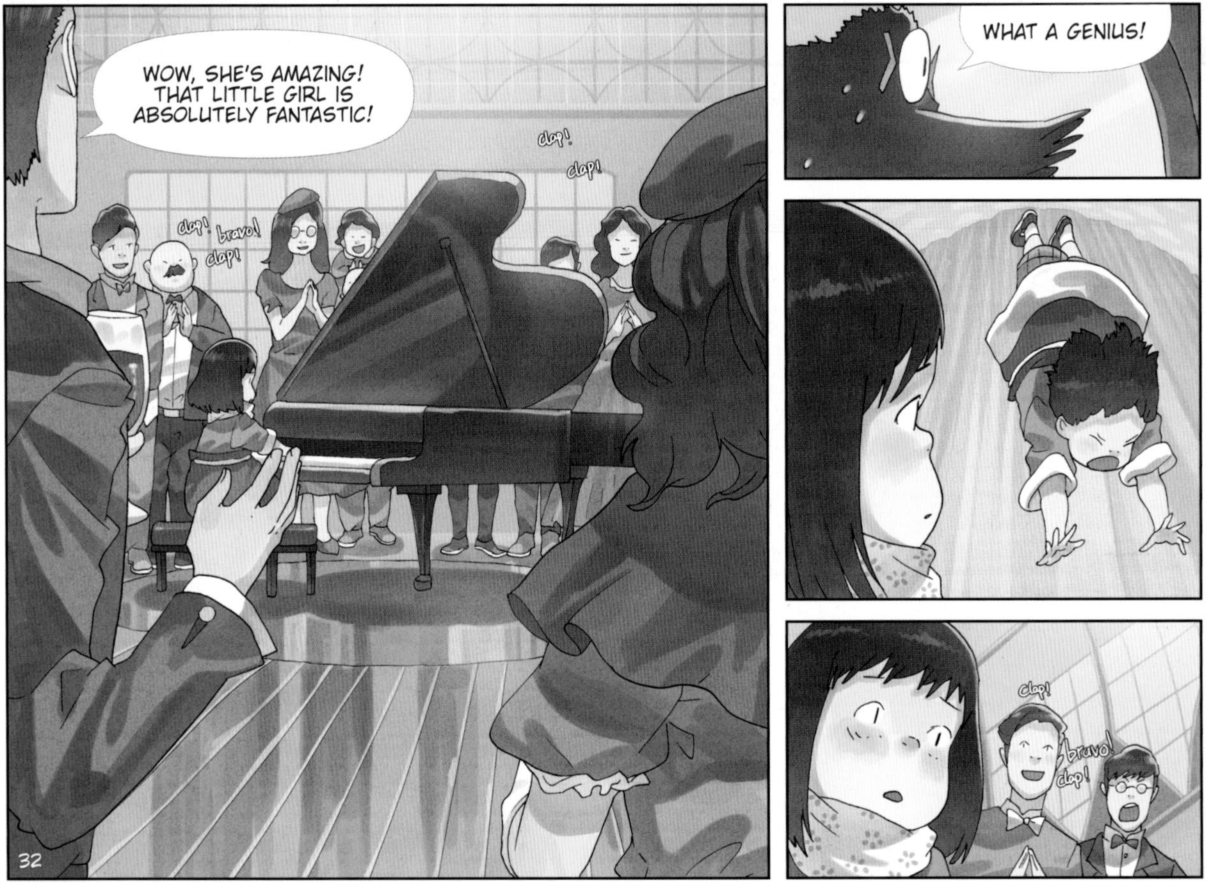
WOW, SHE'S AMAZING! THAT LITTLE GIRL IS ABSOLUTELY FANTASTIC!
clap!
clap!
clap!
bravo!
clap!
WHAT A GENIUS!
clap!
bravo!
clap!

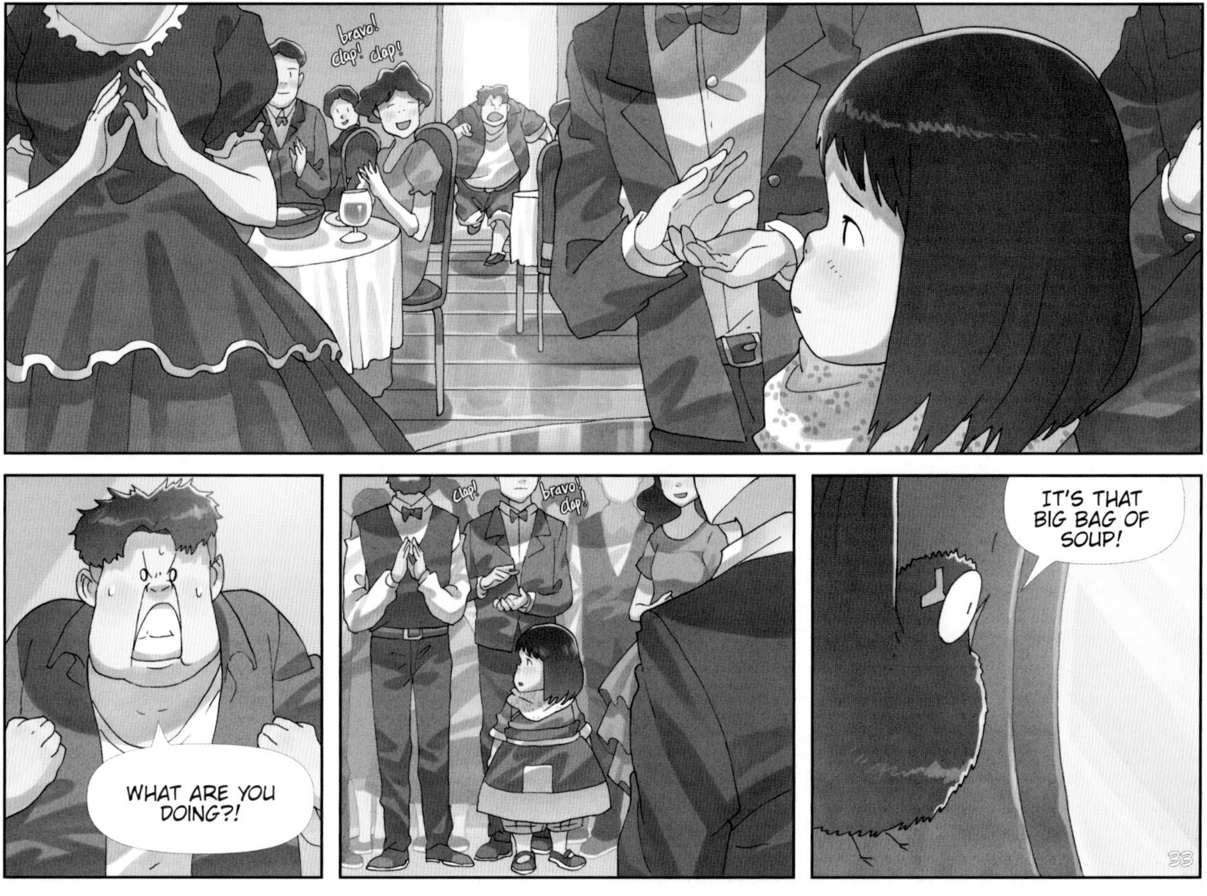
bravo!
clap! clap!
WHAT ARE YOU DOING?!
clap!
bravo! clap!
IT'S THAT BIG BAG OF SOUP!

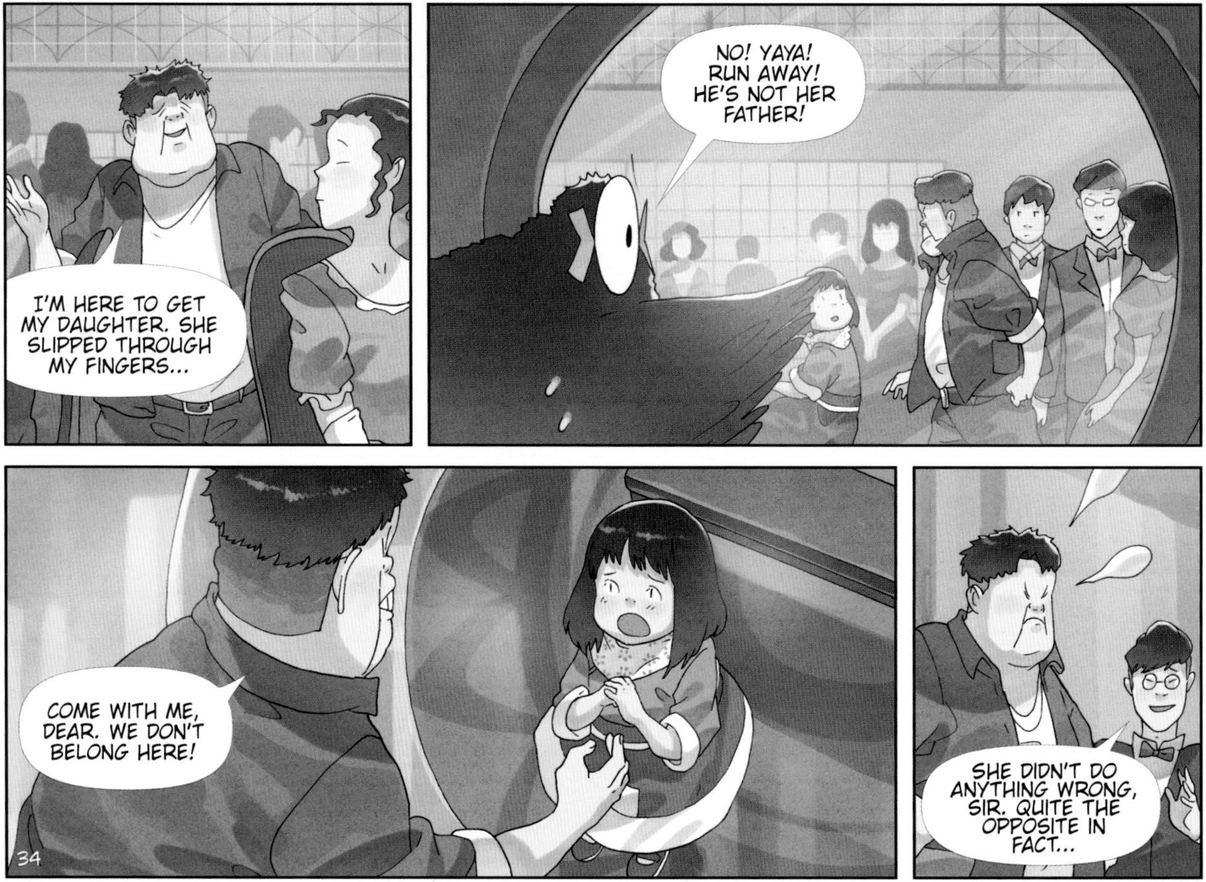
I'M HERE TO GET MY DAUGHTER. SHE SLIPPED THROUGH MY FINGERS...
NO! YAYA! RUN AWAY! HE'S NOT HER FATHER!
COME WITH ME, DEAR. WE DON'T BELONG HERE!
SHE DIDN'T DO ANYTHING WRONG, SIR. QUITE THE OPPOSITE IN FACT...

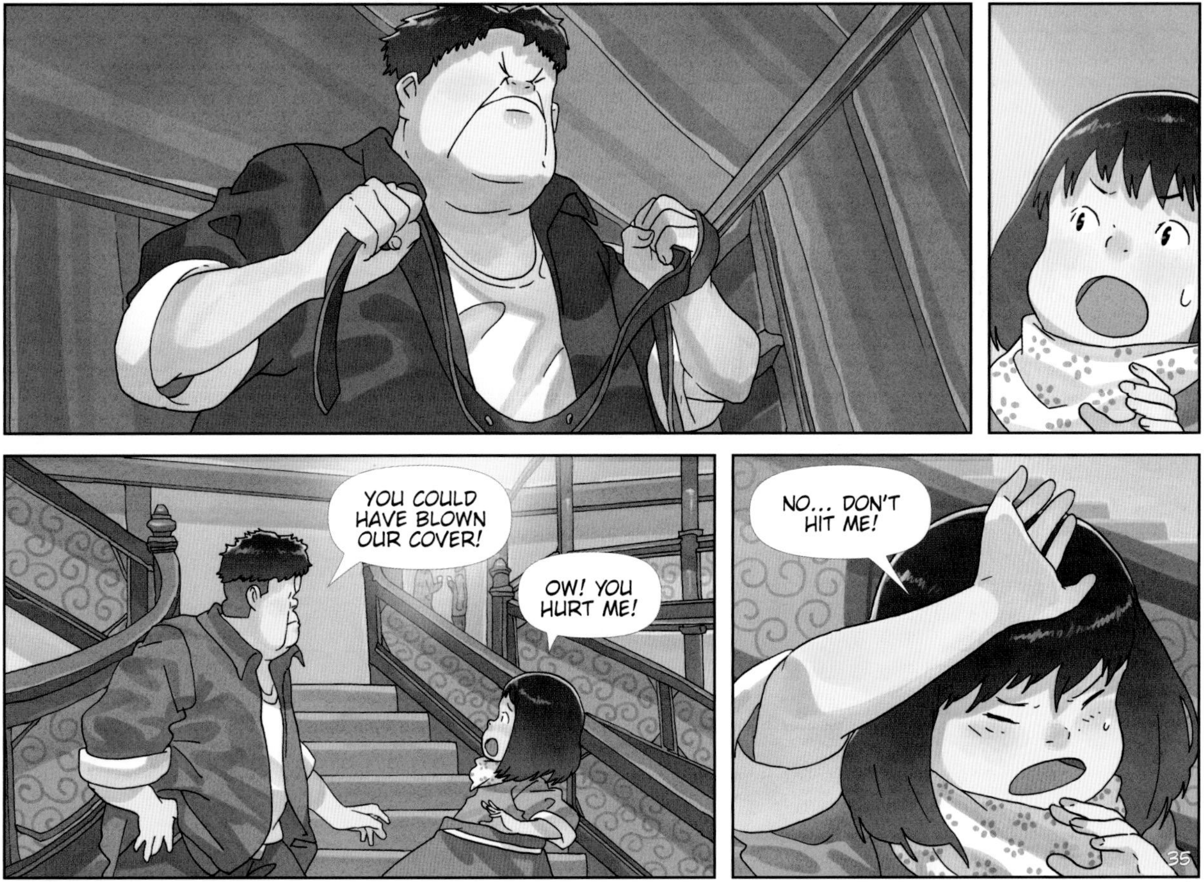
YOU COULD HAVE BLOWN OUR COVER!
OW! YOU HURT ME!
NO... DON'T HIT ME!

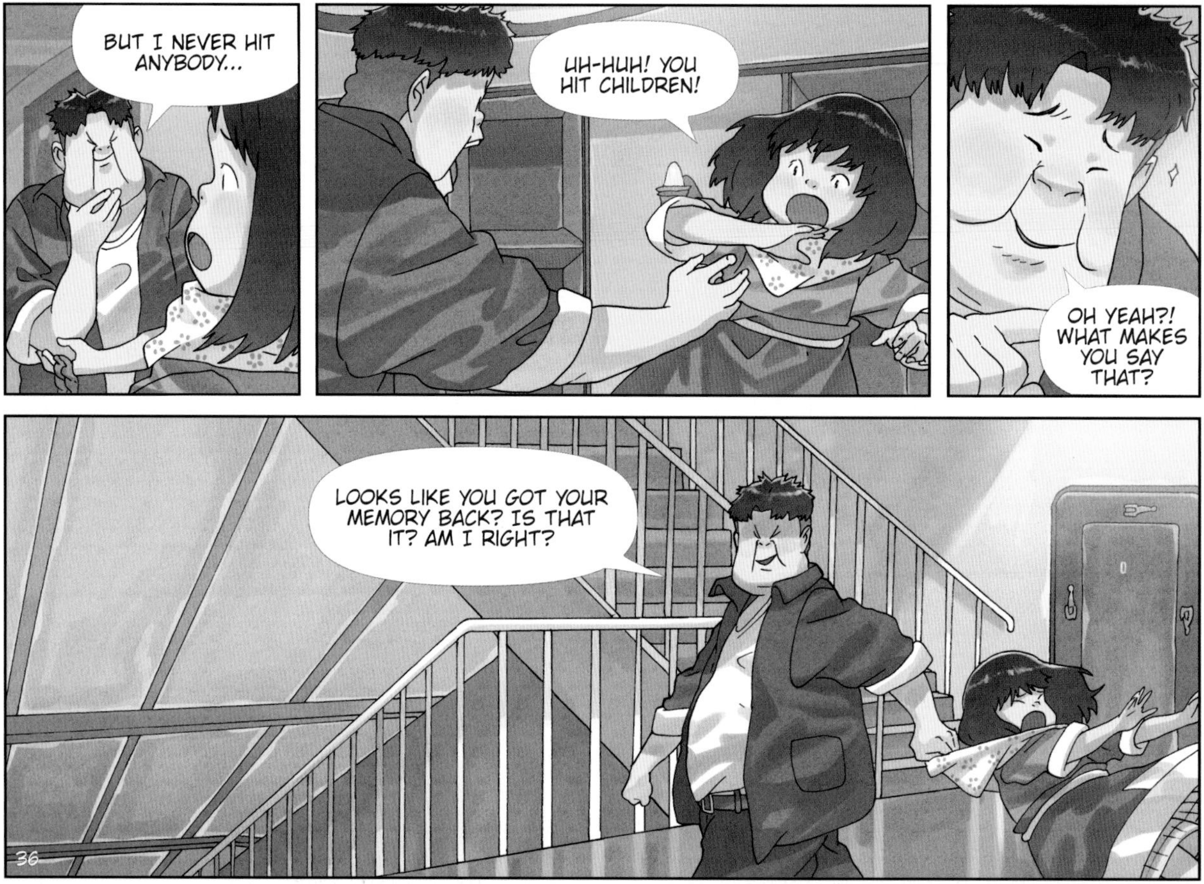
BUT I NEVER HIT ANYBODY...
UH-HUH! YOU HIT CHILDREN!
OH YEAH?! WHAT MAKES YOU SAY THAT?
LOOKS LIKE YOU GOT YOUR MEMORY BACK? IS THAT IT? AM I RIGHT?

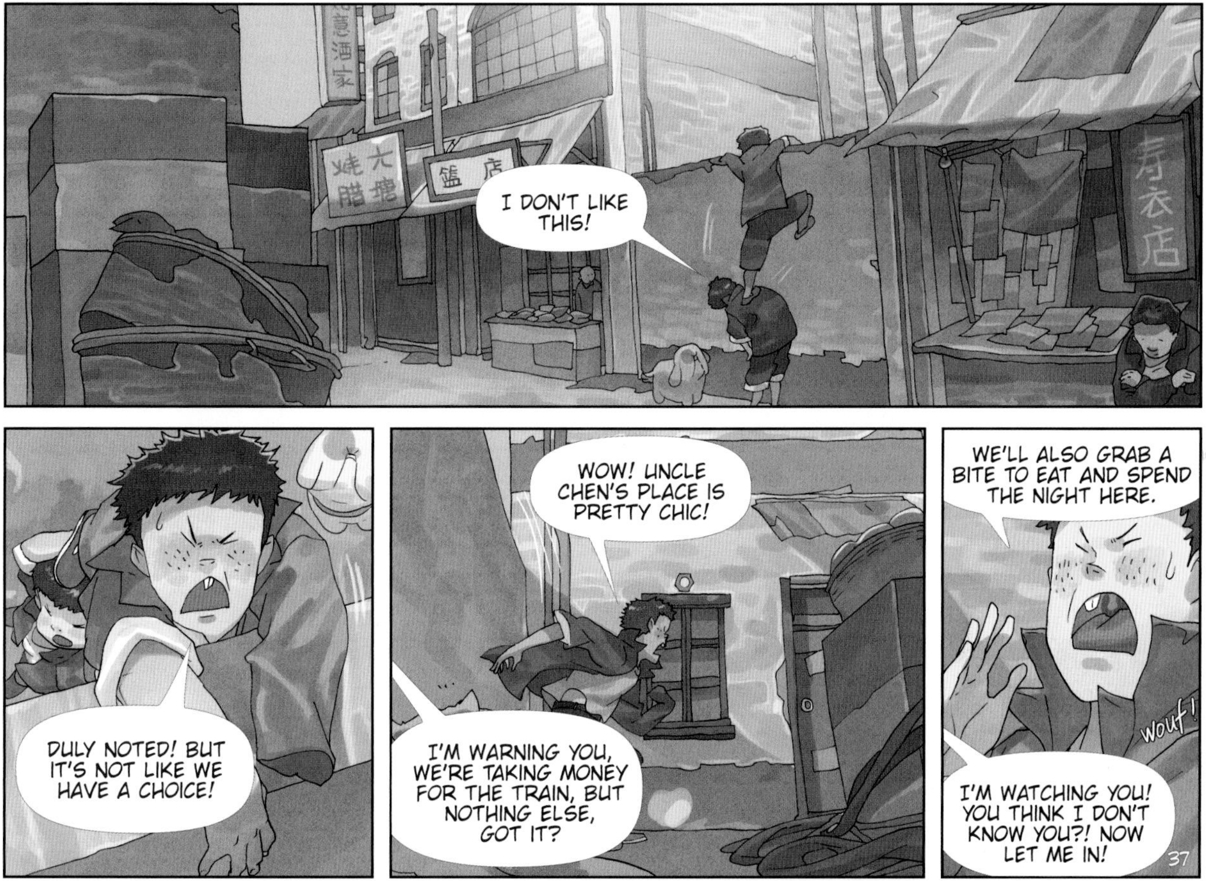
寿衣店
I DON'T LIKE THIS!
DULY NOTED! BUT IT'S NOT LIKE WE HAVE A CHOICE!
WOW! UNCLE CHEN'S PLACE IS PRETTY CHIC!
I'M WARNING YOU, WE'RE TAKING MONEY FOR THE TRAIN, BUT NOTHING ELSE, GOT IT?
WE'LL ALSO GRAB A BITE TO EAT AND SPEND THE NIGHT HERE.
WOUF!
I'M WATCHING YOU! YOU THINK I DON'T KNOW YOU?! NOW LET ME IN!

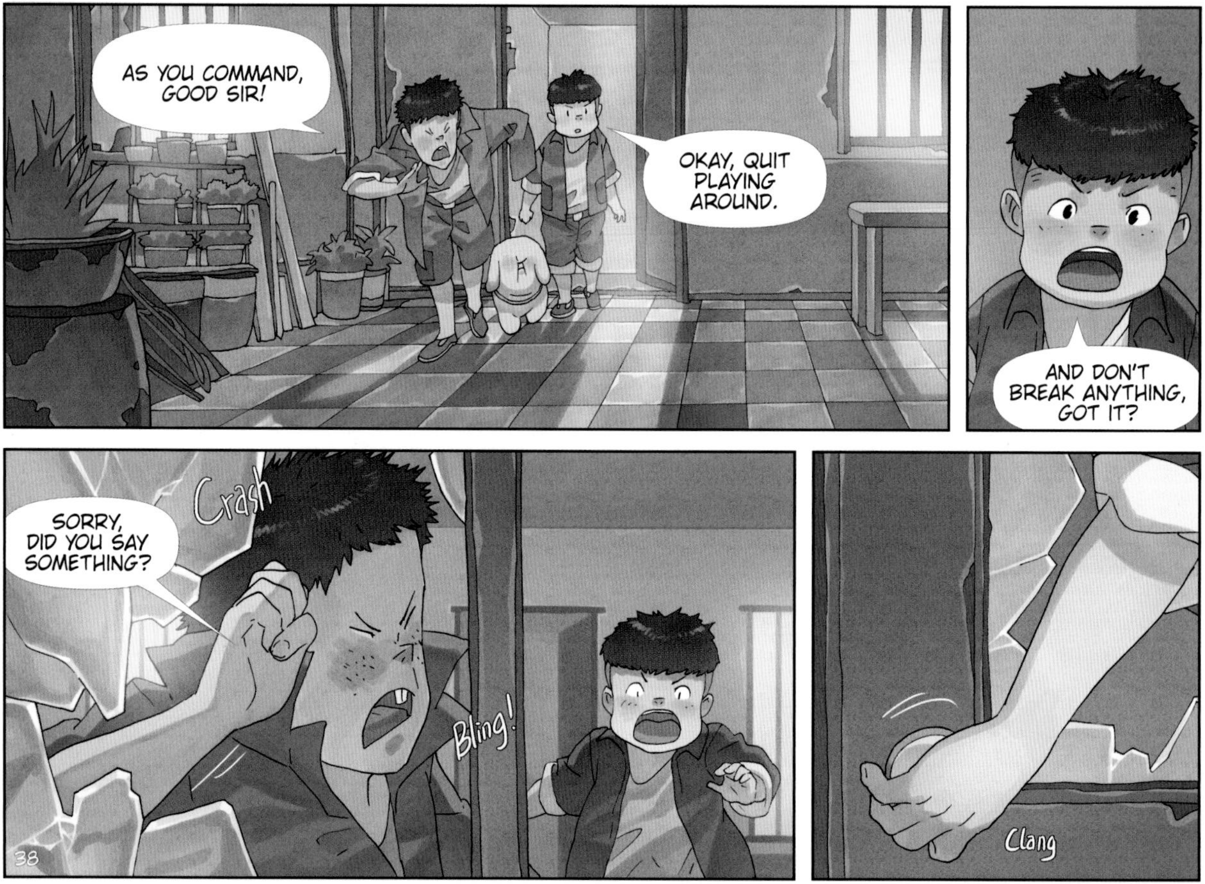
AS YOU COMMAND, GOOD SIR!
OKAY, QUIT PLAYING AROUND.
AND DON'T BREAK ANYTHING, GOT IT?
Crash
SORRY, DID YOU SAY SOMETHING?
Bling!
Clang

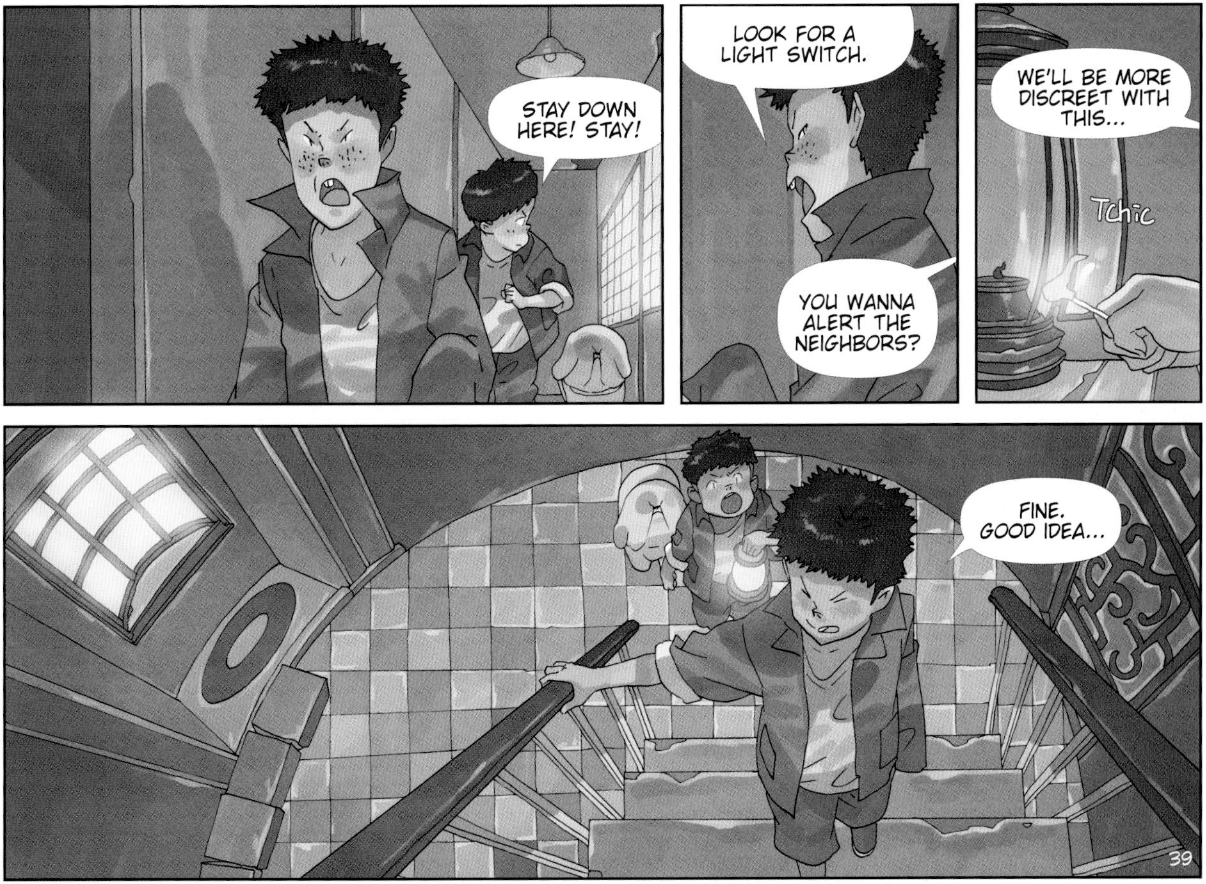
STAY DOWN HERE! STAY!
LOOK FOR A LIGHT SWITCH.
YOU WANNA ALERT THE NEIGHBORS?
WE'LL BE MORE DISCREET WITH THIS...
Tchic
FINE. GOOD IDEA...

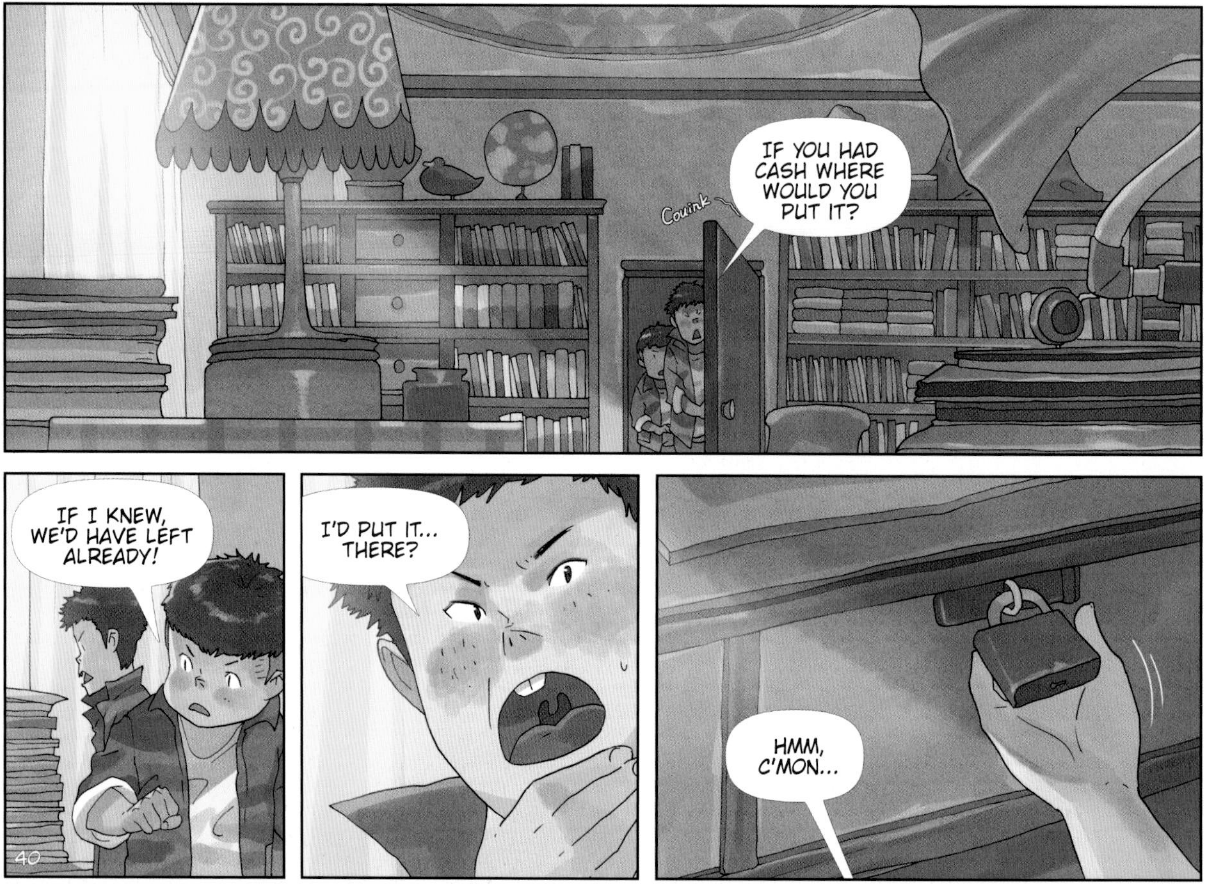
Couink
IF YOU HAD CASH WHERE WOULD YOU PUT IT?
IF I KNEW, WE'D HAVE LEFT ALREADY!
I'D PUT IT... THERE?
HMM, C'MON...

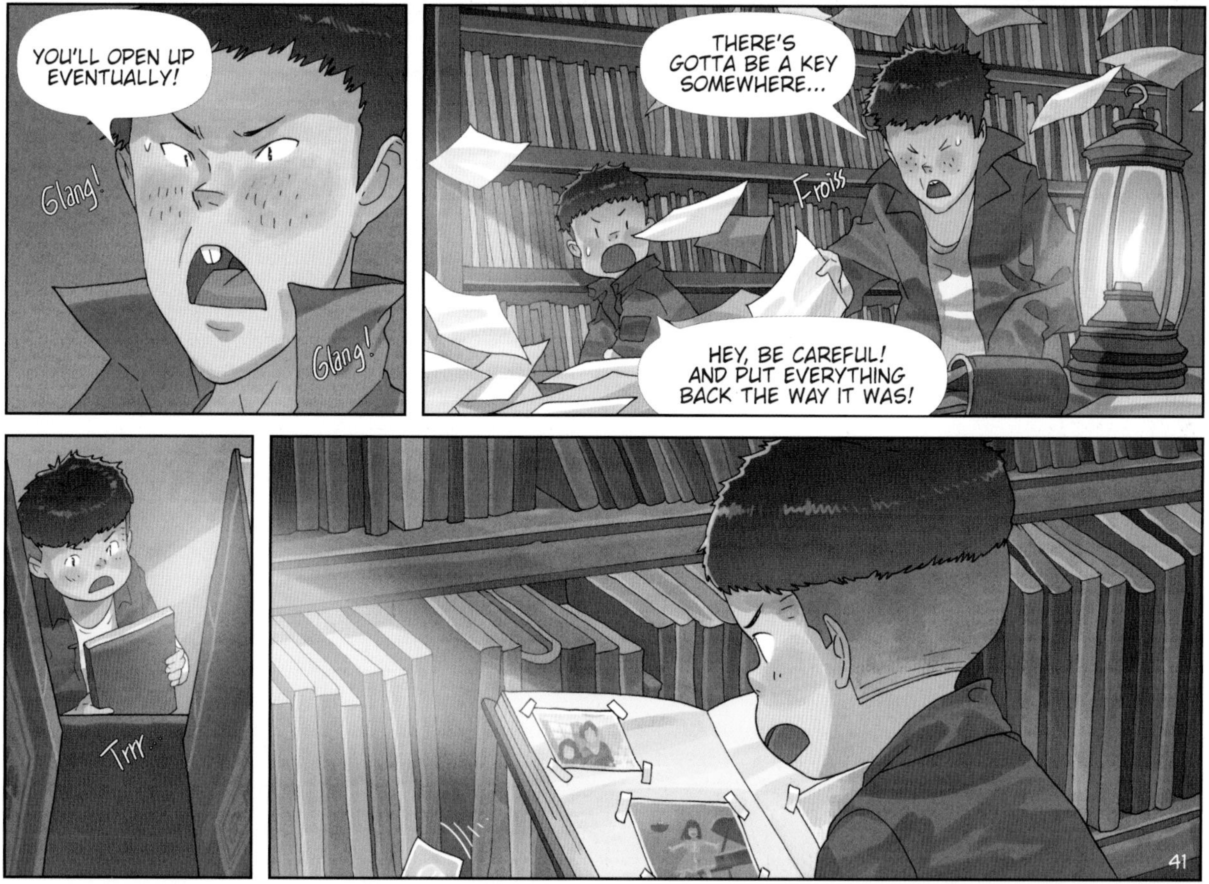
YOU'LL OPEN UP EVENTUALLY!
Glang!
Glang!
THERE'S GOTTA BE A KEY SOMEWHERE...
Froiss
HEY, BE CAREFUL! AND PUT EVERYTHING BACK THE WAY IT WAS!
Trrr...

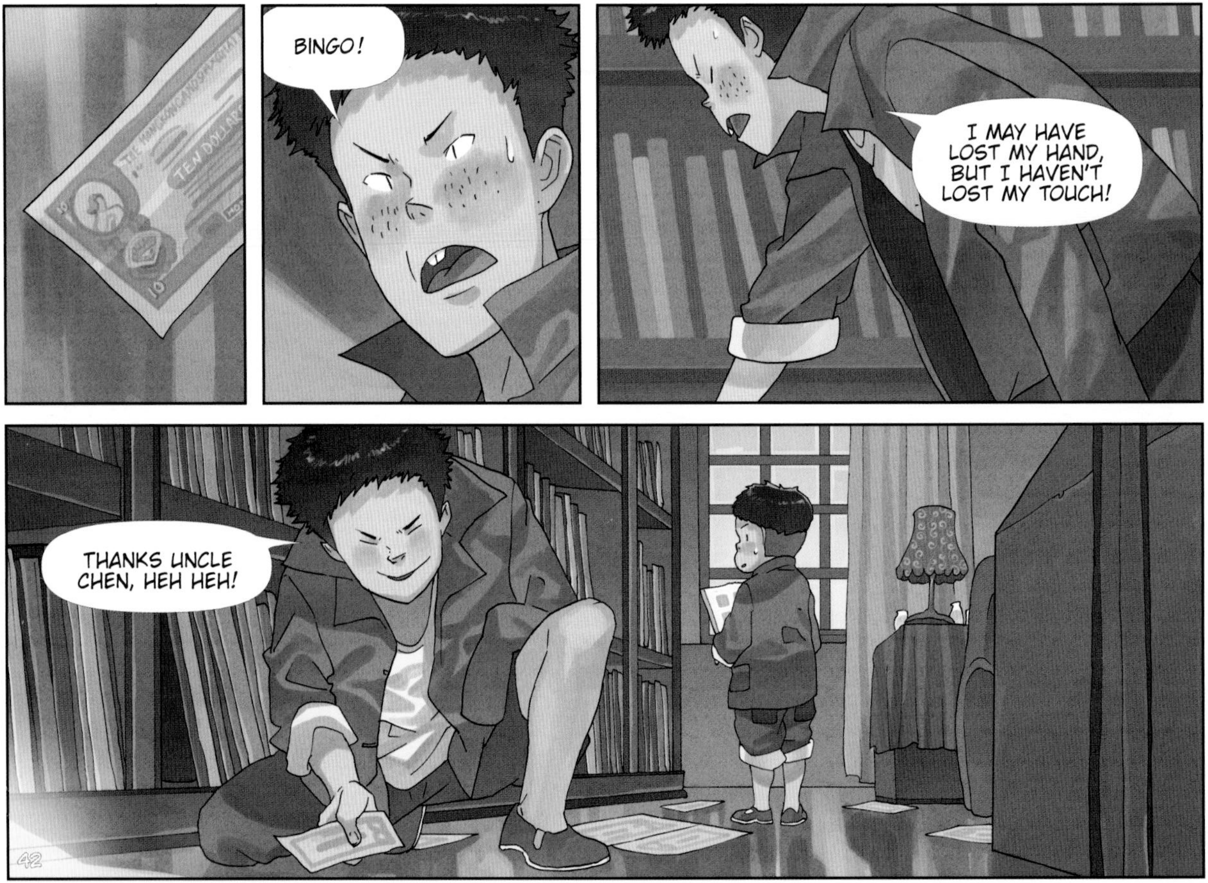
BINGO!
I MAY HAVE LOST MY HAND, BUT I HAVEN'T LOST MY TOUCH!
THANKS UNCLE CHEN, HEH HEH!

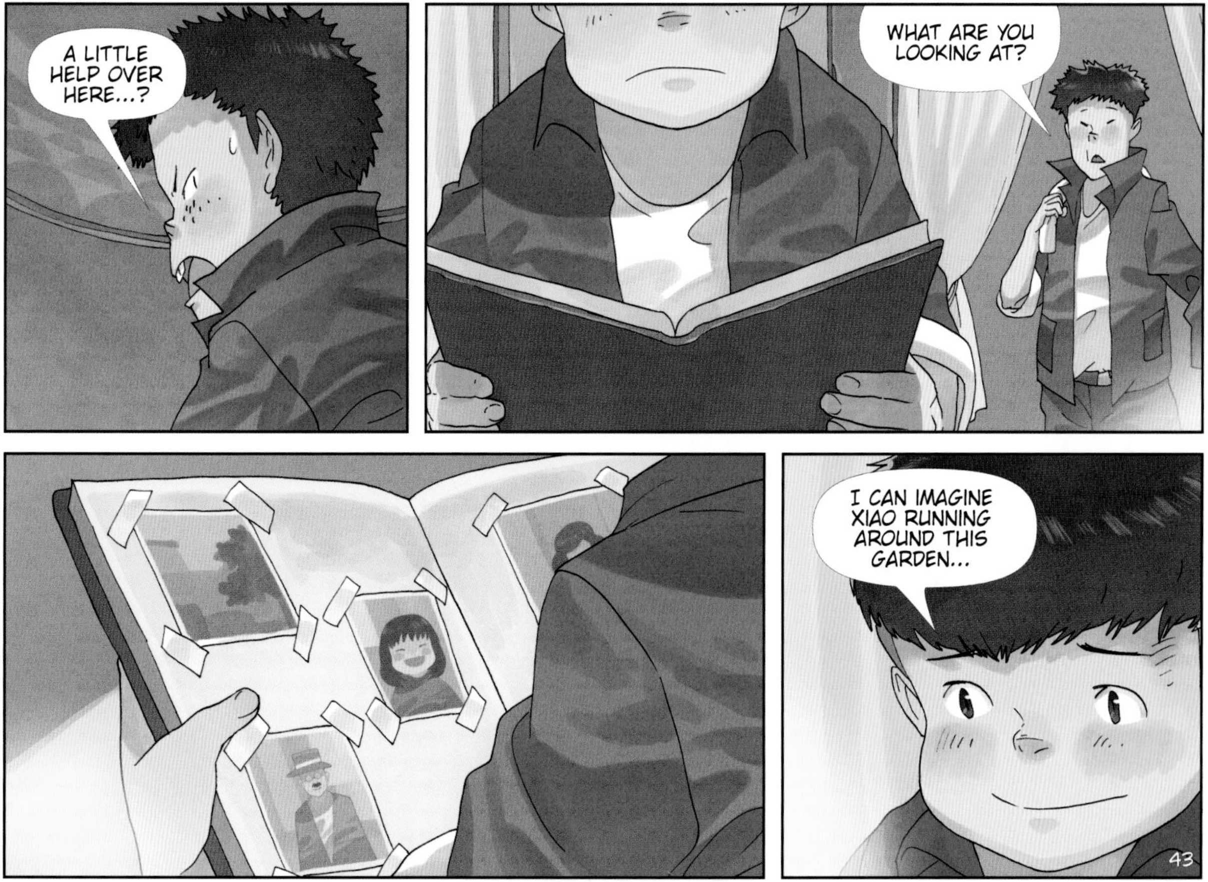

A LITTLE HELP OVER HERE...?
WHAT ARE YOU LOOKING AT?
I CAN IMAGINE XIAO RUNNING AROUND THIS GARDEN...

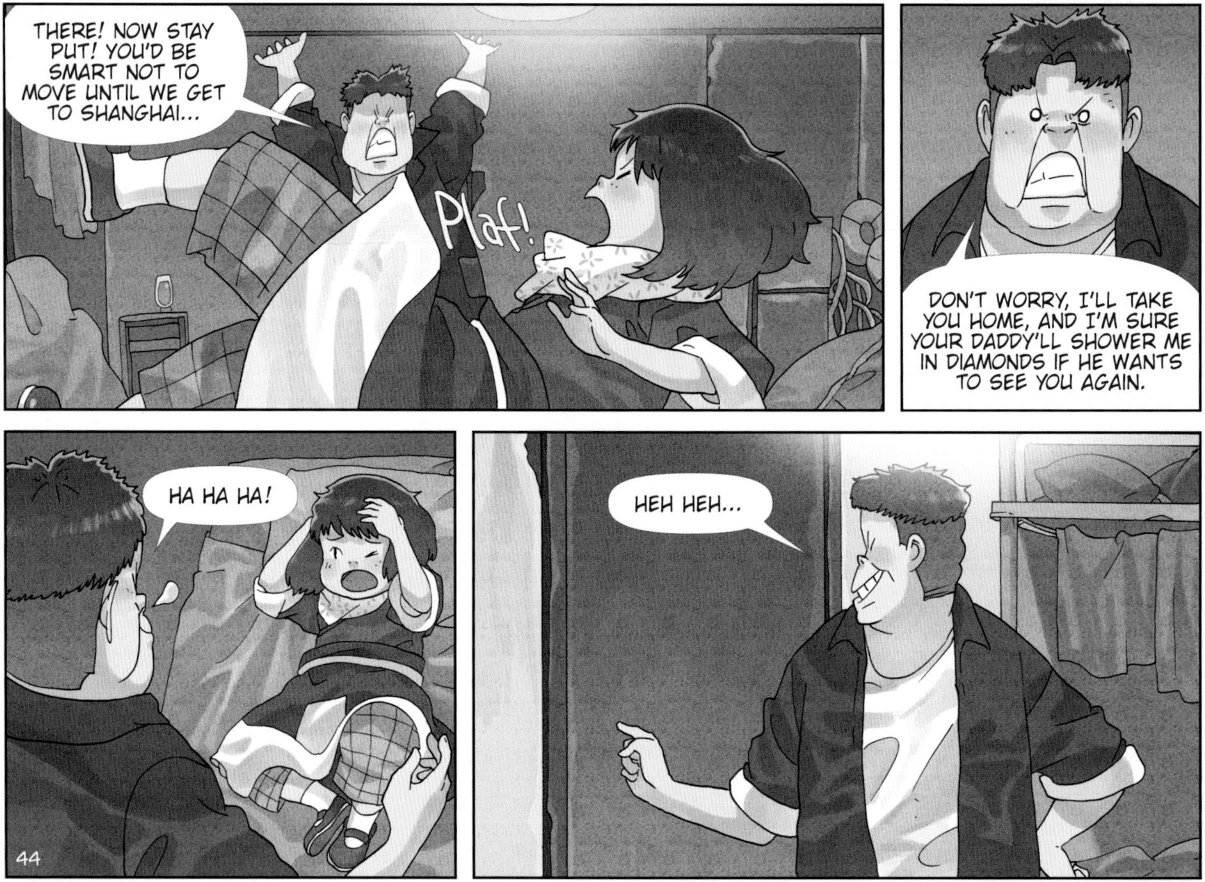
THERE! NOW STAY PUT! YOU'D BE SMART NOT TO MOVE UNTIL WE GET TO SHANGHAI...
Plaf!
DON'T WORRY, I'LL TAKE YOU HOME, AND I'M SURE YOUR DADDY'LL SHOWER ME IN DIAMONDS IF HE WANTS TO SEE YOU AGAIN.
HA HA HA!
HEH HEH...

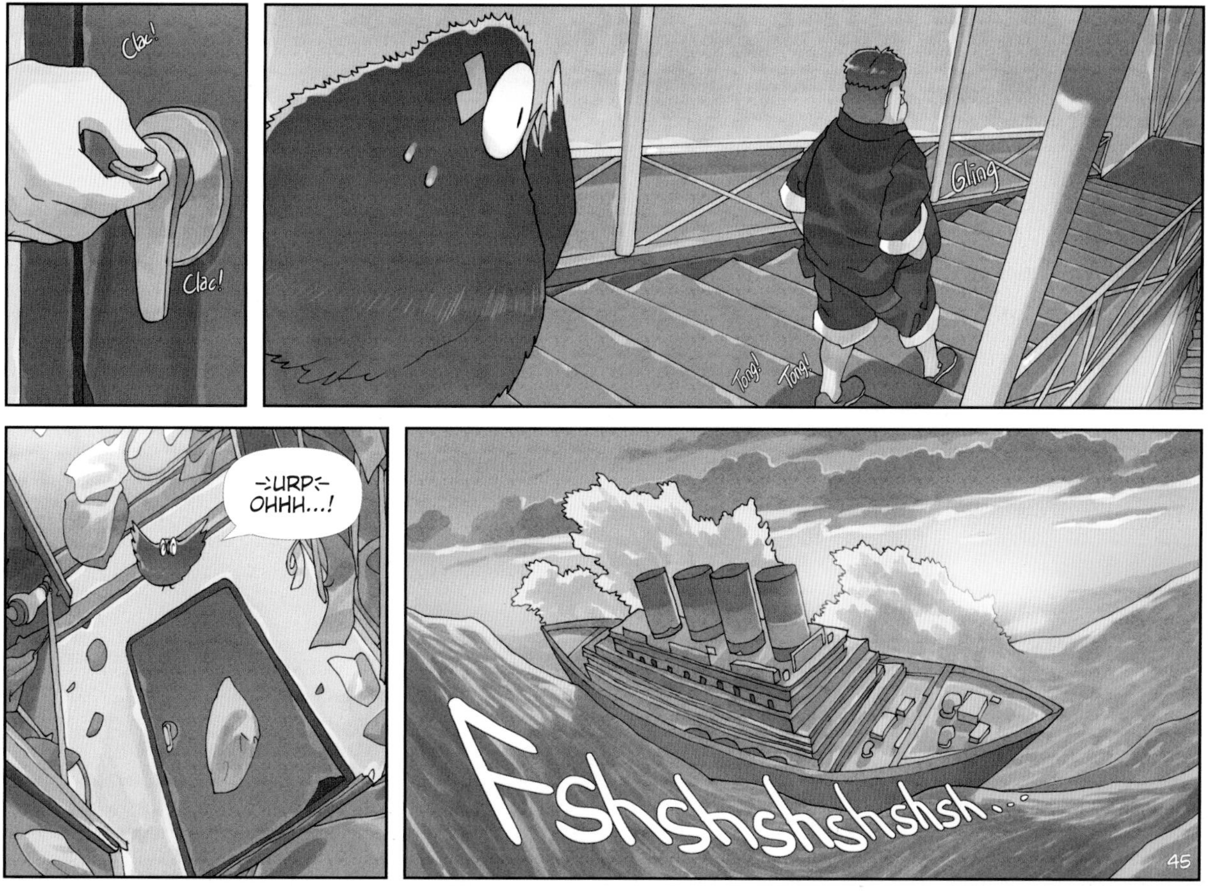
Clac!
Clac!
Gling
Tong!
Tong!
URP
OHHH...!
Fshshshshshsh..

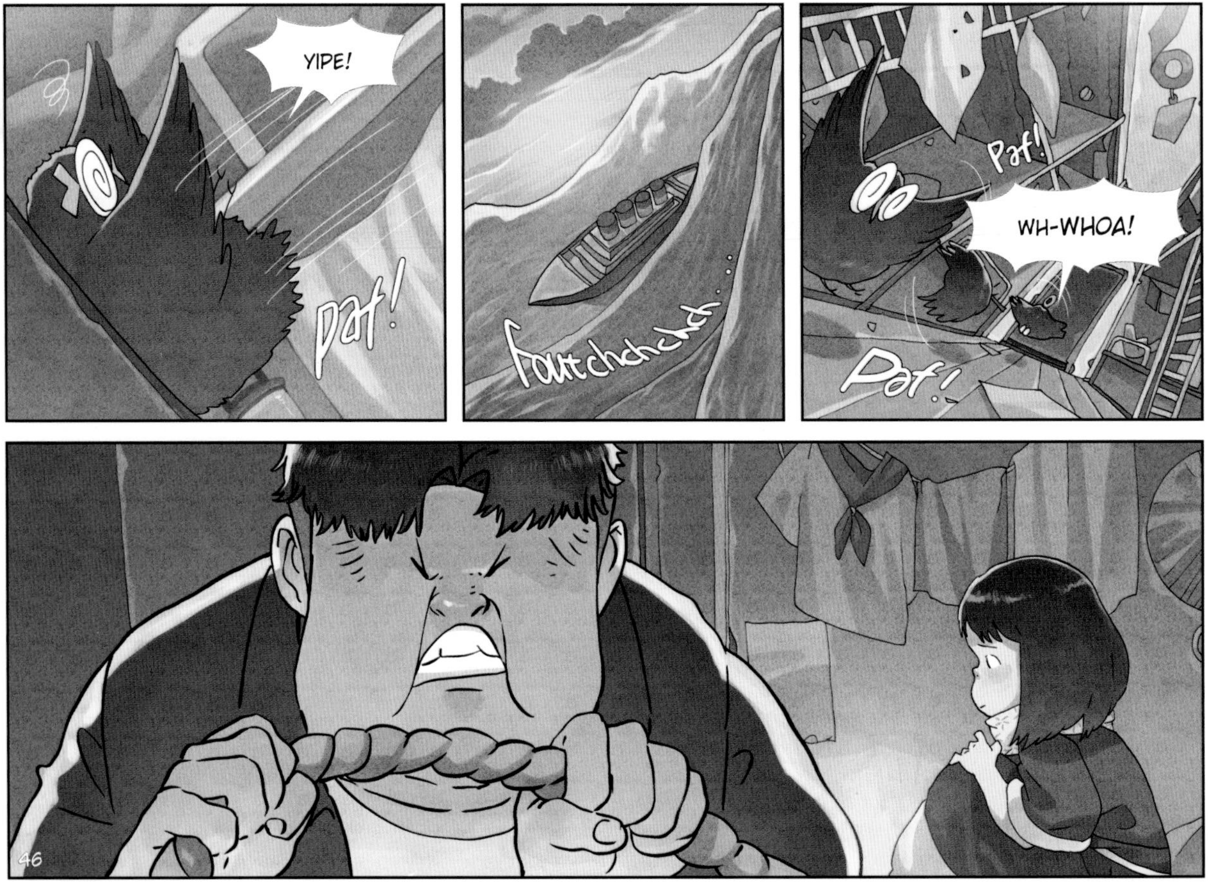
YIPE!
Paf!
Fautchchchch...
Paf!
WH-WHOA!
Paf!

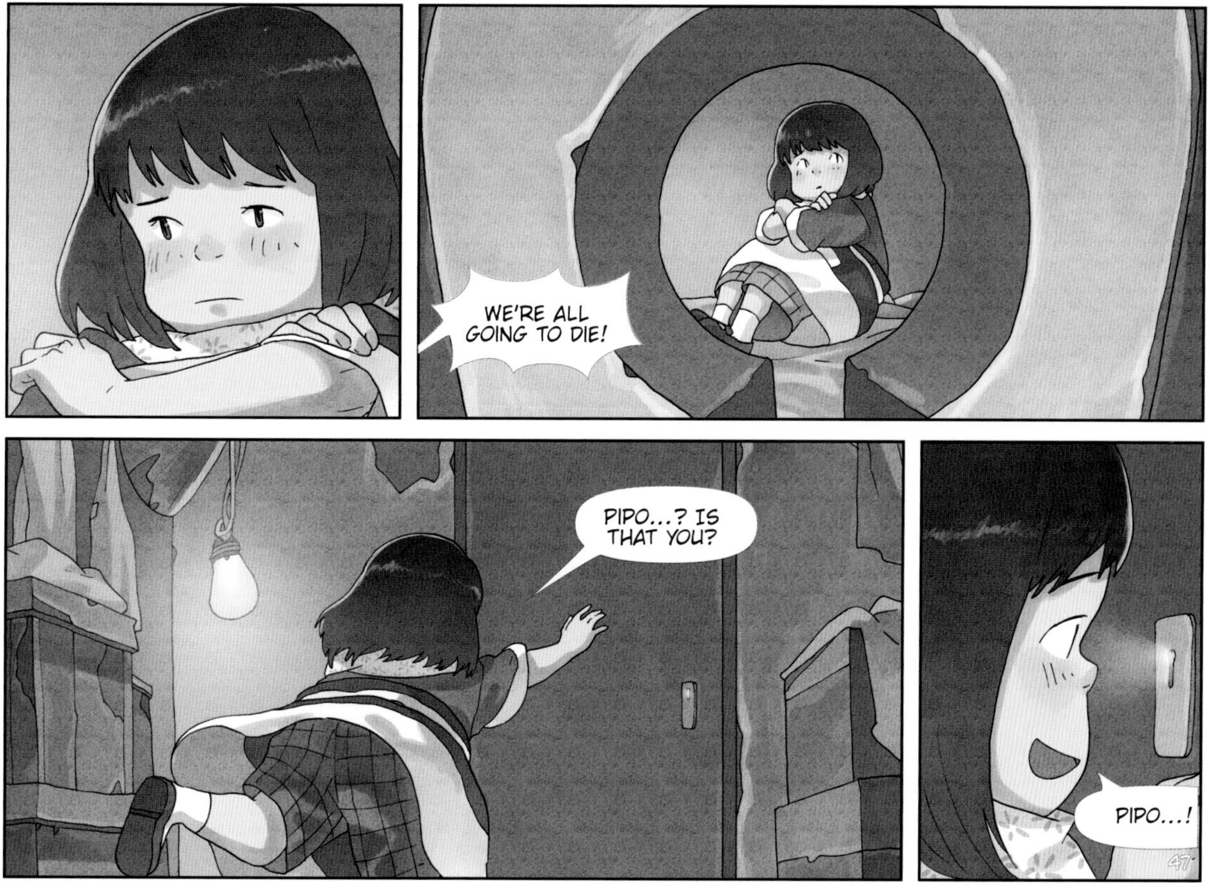
WE'RE ALL GOING TO DIE!
PIPO...? IS THAT YOU?
PIPO...!

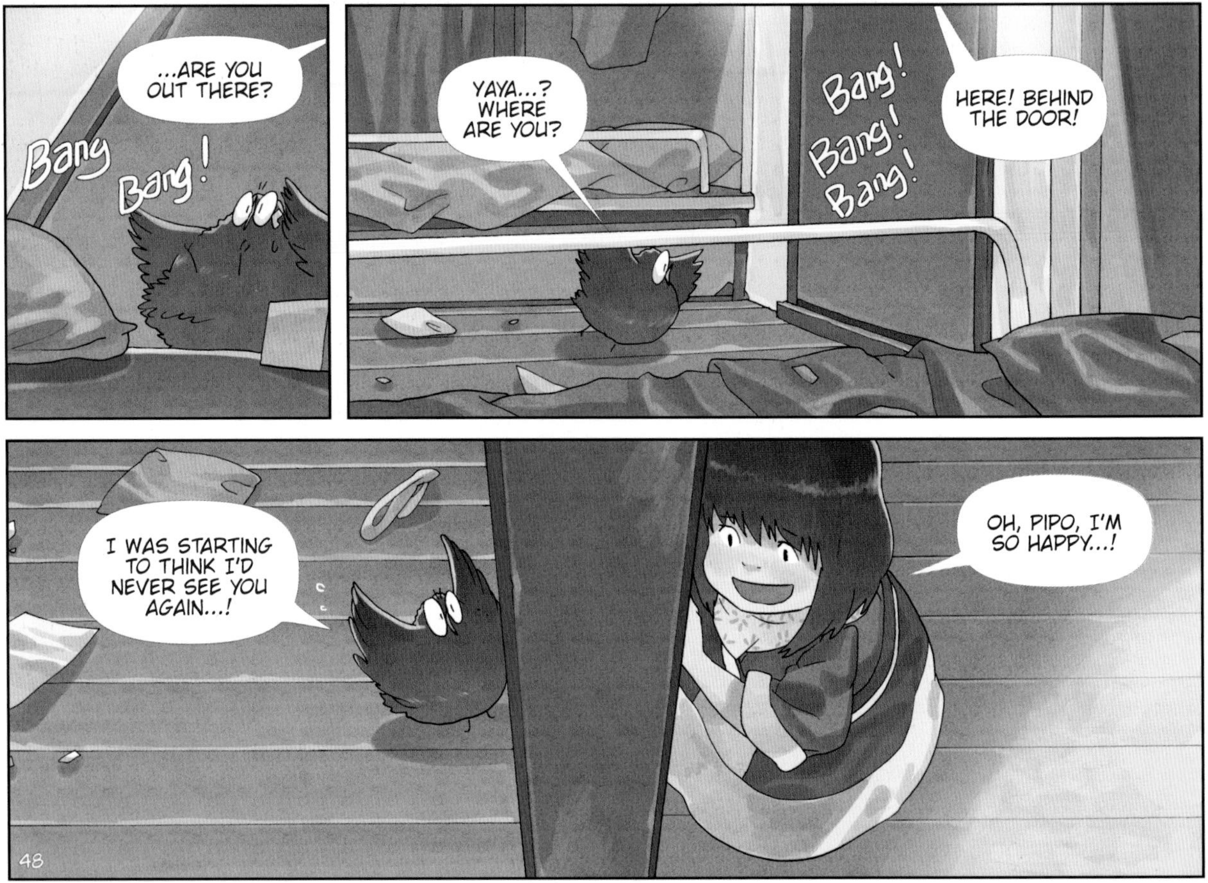
...ARE YOU OUT THERE?
Bang Bang!
YAYA...? WHERE ARE YOU?
Bang! Bang! Bang!
HERE! BEHIND THE DOOR!
I WAS STARTING TO THINK I'D NEVER SEE YOU AGAIN...!
OH, PIPO, I'M SO HAPPY...!

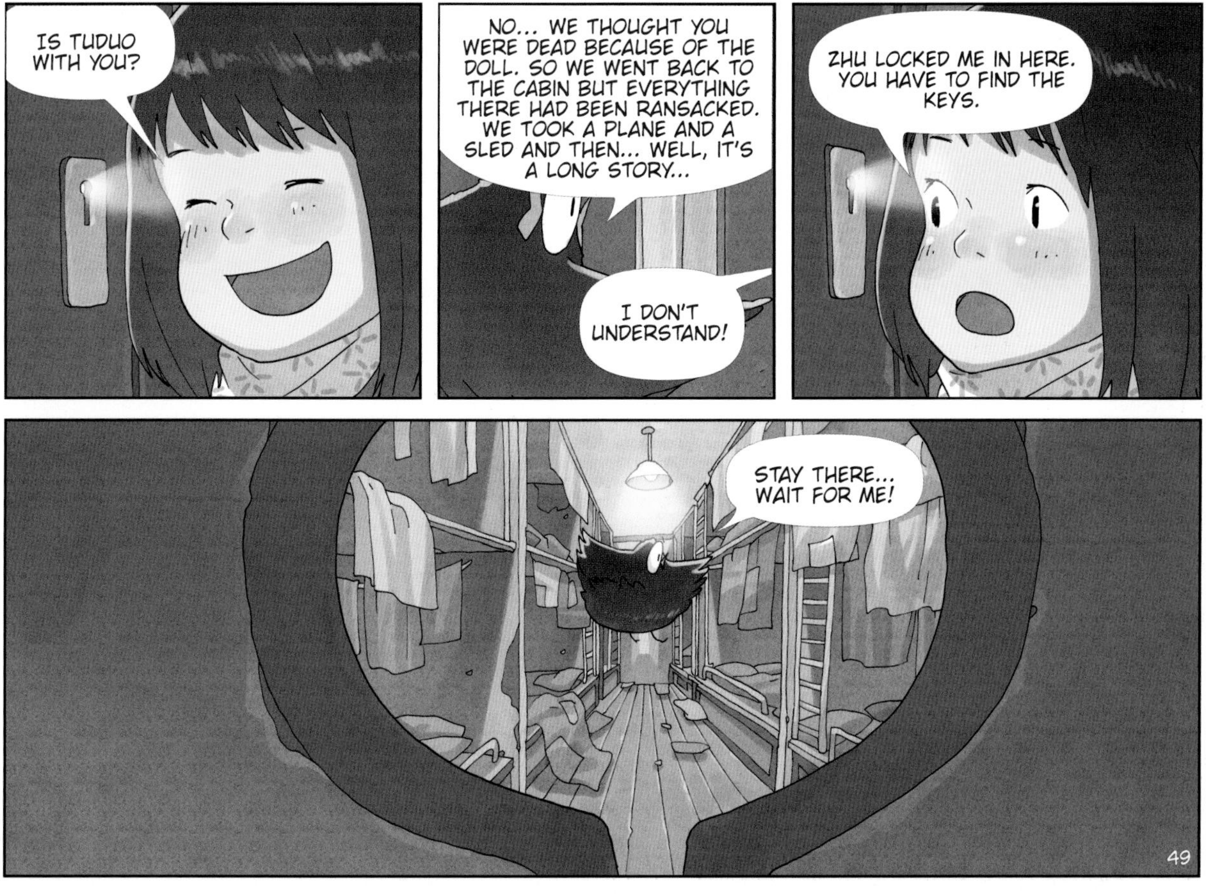
IS TUDUO WITH YOU?
NO... WE THOUGHT YOU WERE DEAD BECAUSE OF THE DOLL. SO WE WENT BACK TO THE CABIN BUT EVERYTHING THERE HAD BEEN RANSACKED. WE TOOK A PLANE AND A SLED AND THEN... WELL, IT'S A LONG STORY...
I DON'T UNDERSTAND!
ZHU LOCKED ME IN HERE. YOU HAVE TO FIND THE KEYS.
STAY THERE... WAIT FOR ME!

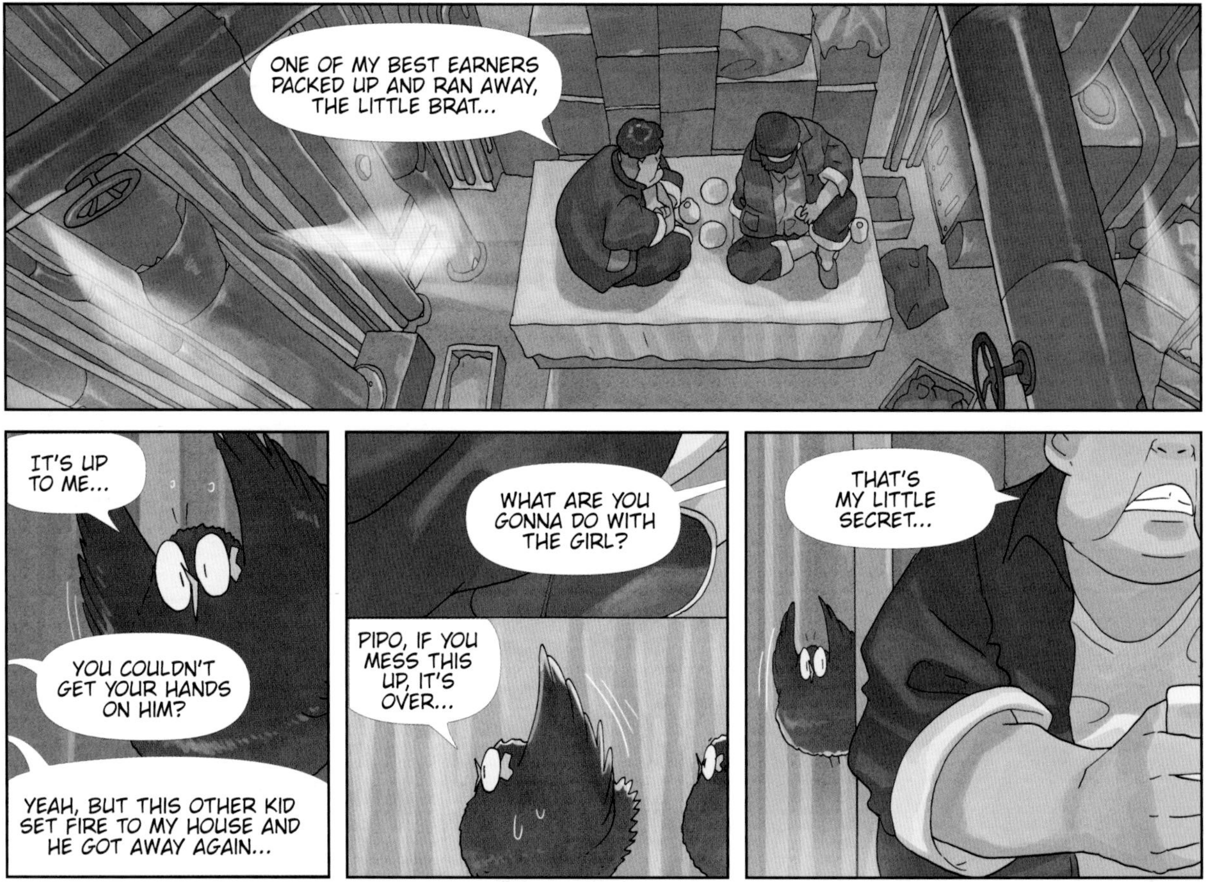
ONE OF MY BEST EARNERS PACKED UP AND RAN AWAY, THE LITTLE BRAT...
IT'S UP TO ME...
YOU COULDN'T GET YOUR HANDS ON HIM?
YEAH, BUT THIS OTHER KID SET FIRE TO MY HOUSE AND HE GOT AWAY AGAIN...
WHAT ARE YOU GONNA DO WITH THE GIRL?
PIPO, IF YOU MESS THIS UP, IT'S OVER...
THAT'S MY LITTLE SECRET...

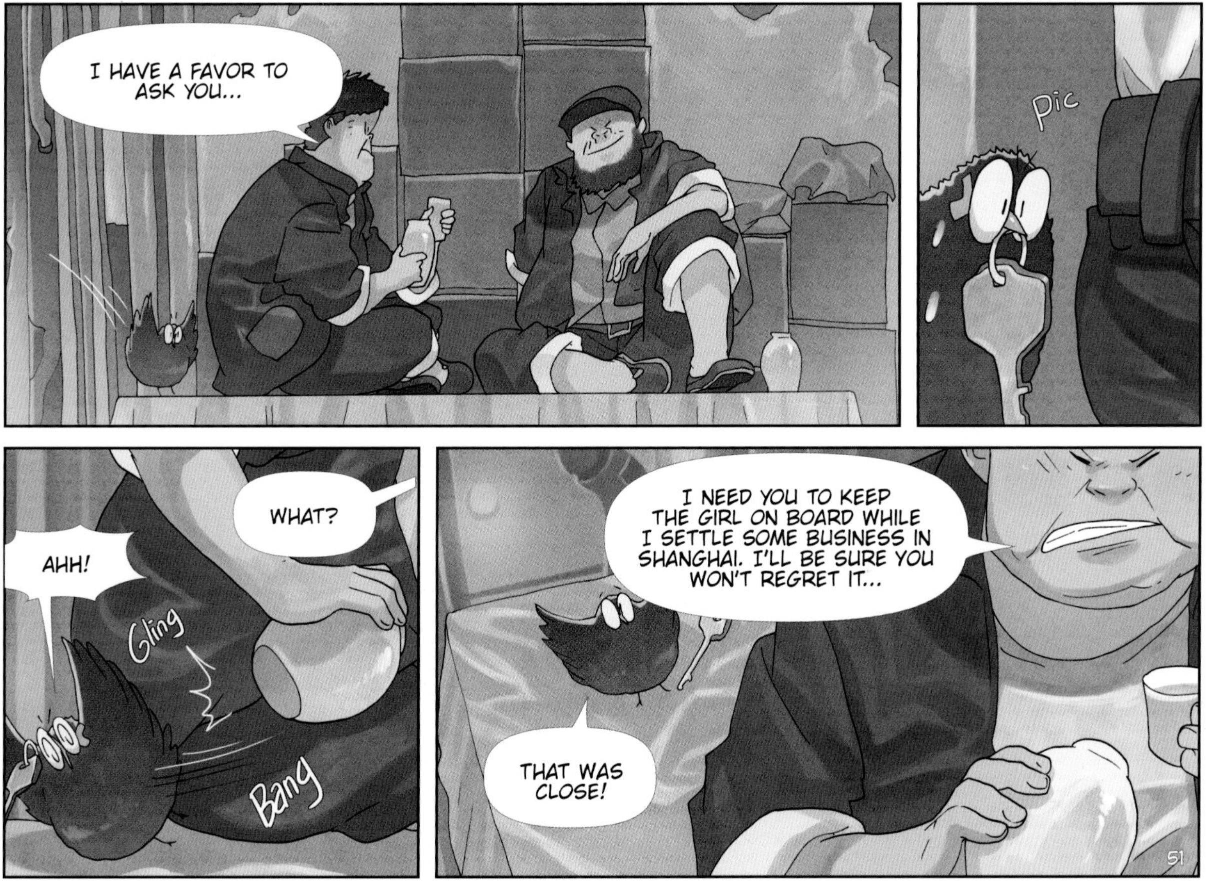
I HAVE A FAVOR TO ASK YOU...
Pic
WHAT?
AHH!
Gling
Bang
I NEED YOU TO KEEP THE GIRL ON BOARD WHILE I SETTLE SOME BUSINESS IN SHANGHAI. I'LL BE SURE YOU WON'T REGRET IT...
THAT WAS CLOSE!

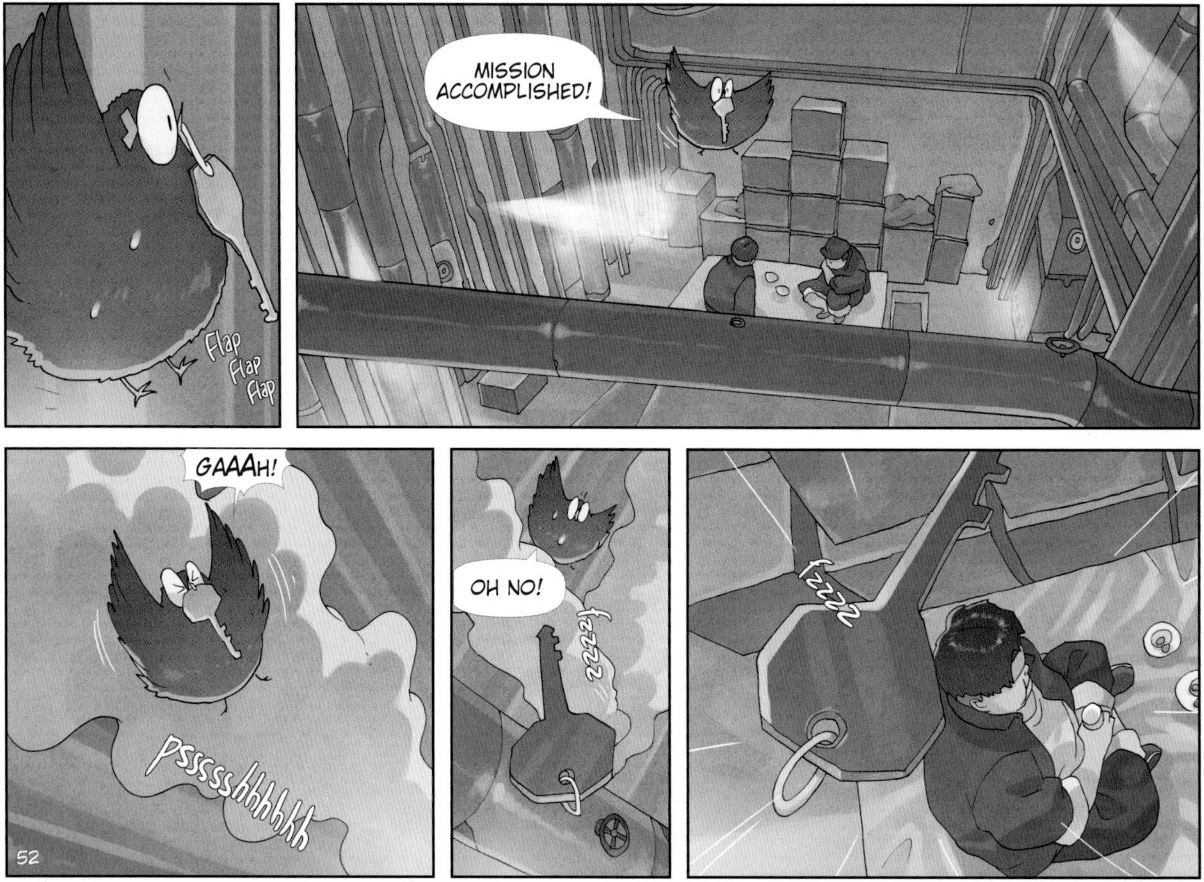
Flap
Flap
Flap
MISSION ACCOMPLISHED!
GAAAH!
Psssssshhhhhh
OH NO!
fzzzz
fzzzz

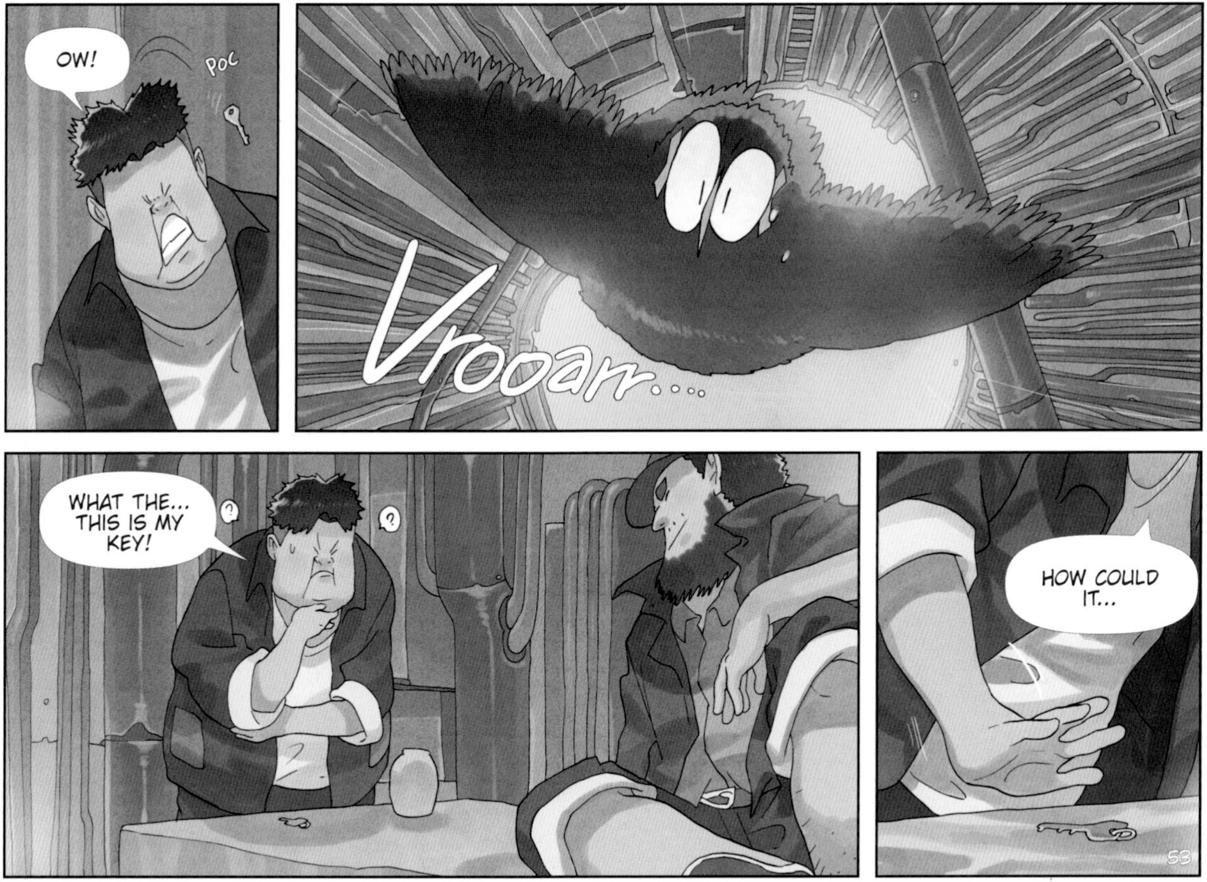
OW!
POC
Vrooarr....
WHAT THE... THIS IS MY KEY!
?
?
HOW COULD IT...

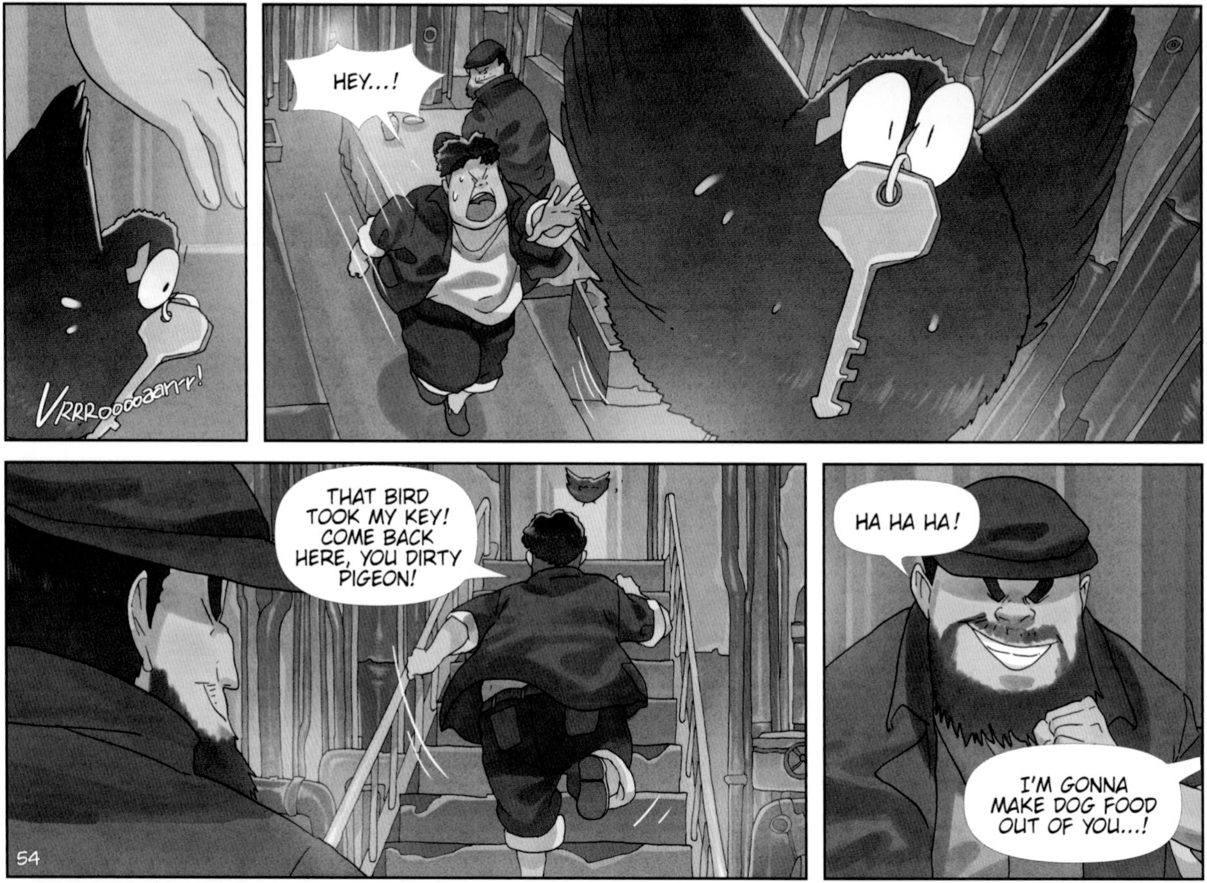
VRRRooooaan-r!
HEY...!
THAT BIRD TOOK MY KEY! COME BACK HERE, YOU DIRTY PIGEON!
HA HA HA!
I'M GONNA MAKE DOG FOOD OUT OF YOU...!

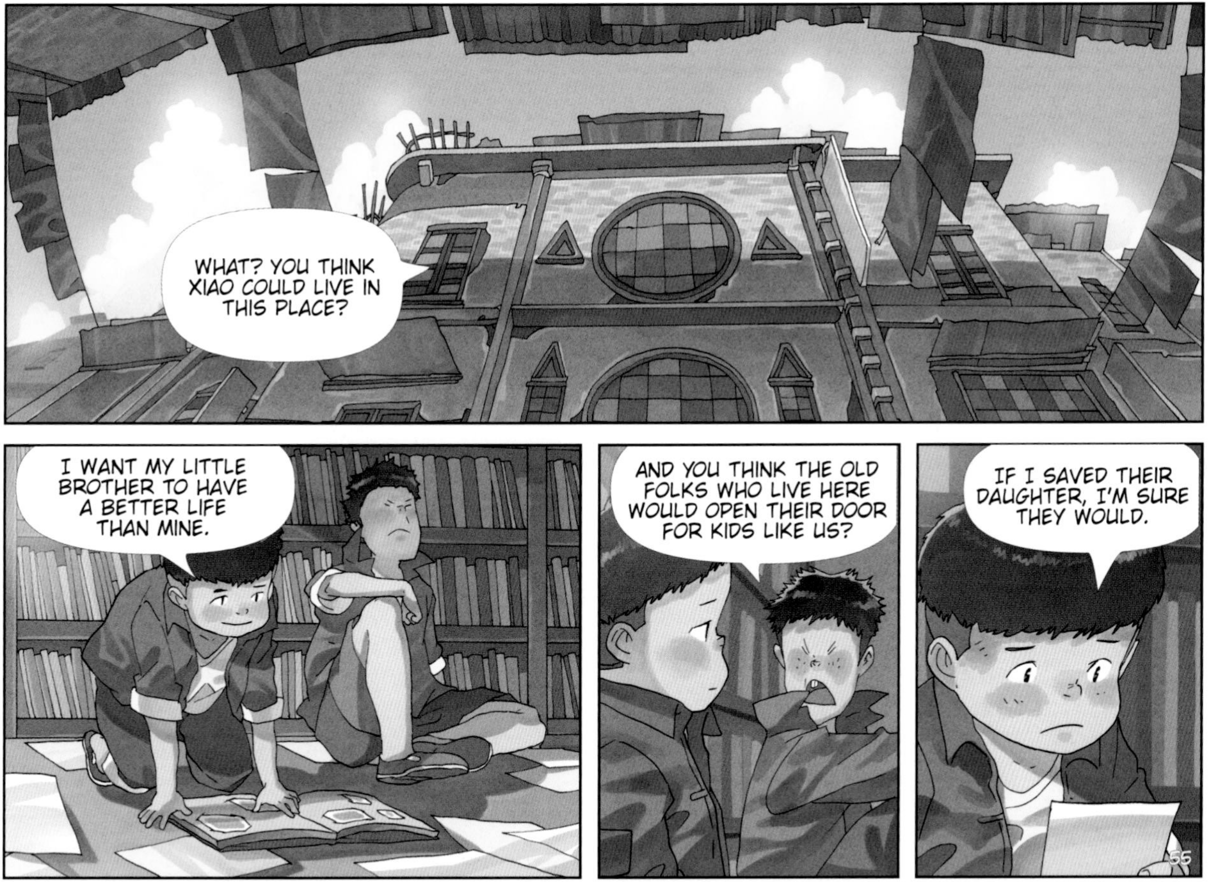
WHAT? YOU THINK XIAO COULD LIVE IN THIS PLACE?
I WANT MY LITTLE BROTHER TO HAVE A BETTER LIFE THAN MINE.
AND YOU THINK THE OLD FOLKS WHO LIVE HERE WOULD OPEN THEIR DOOR FOR KIDS LIKE US?
IF I SAVED THEIR DAUGHTER, I'M SURE THEY WOULD.

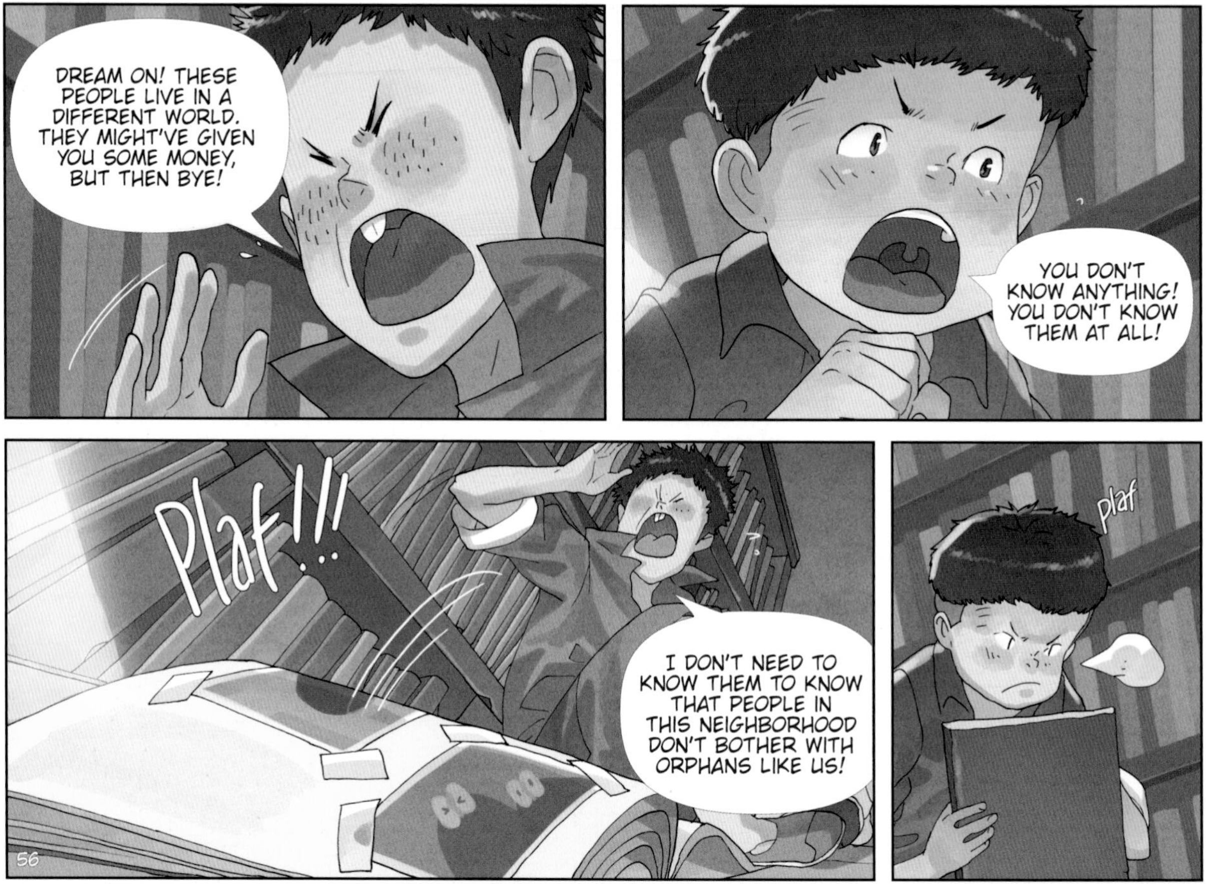
DREAM ON! THESE PEOPLE LIVE IN A DIFFERENT WORLD. THEY MIGHT'VE GIVEN YOU SOME MONEY, BUT THEN BYE!
YOU DON'T KNOW ANYTHING! YOU DON'T KNOW THEM AT ALL!
Plaf!!!
I DON'T NEED TO KNOW THEM TO KNOW THAT PEOPLE IN THIS NEIGHBORHOOD DON'T BOTHER WITH ORPHANS LIKE US!
plaf

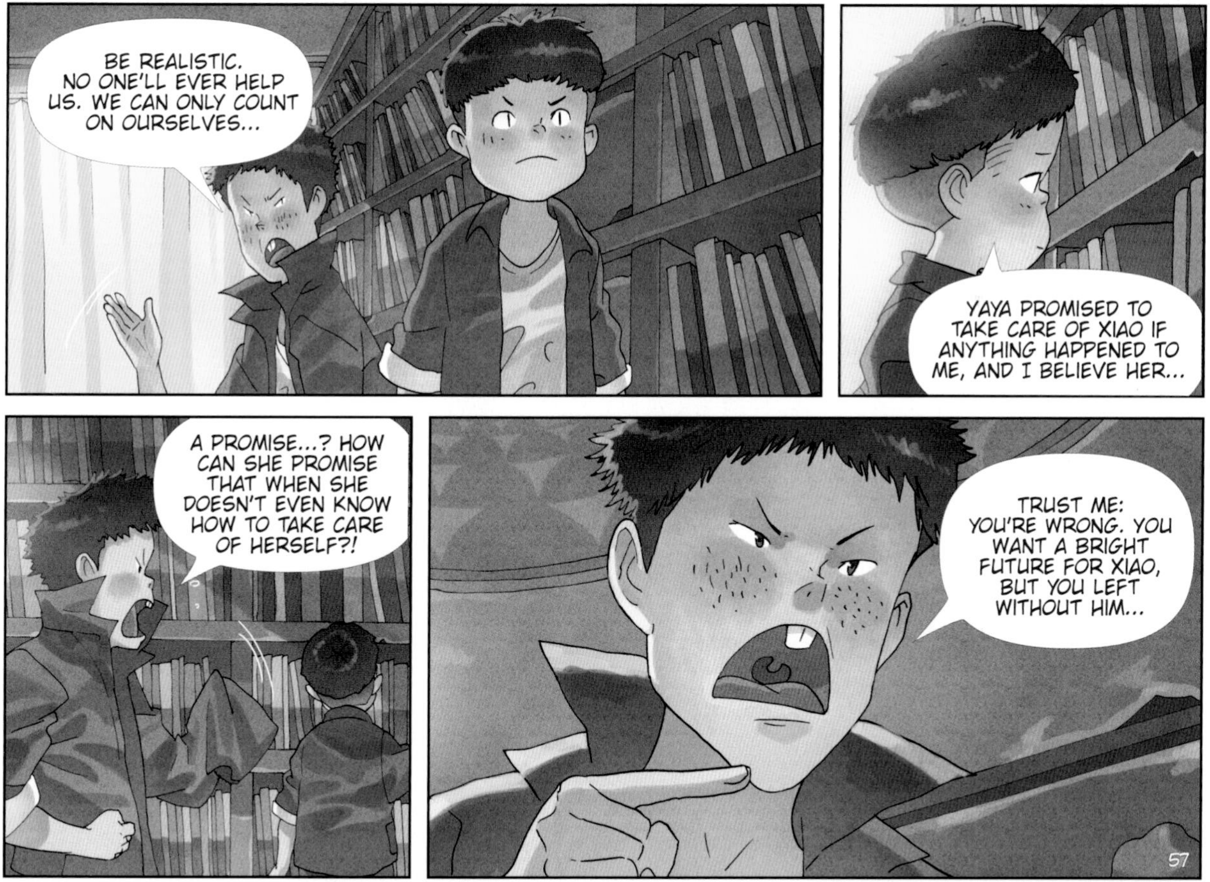
BE REALISTIC. NO ONE'LL EVER HELP US. WE CAN ONLY COUNT ON OURSELVES...
YAYA PROMISED TO TAKE CARE OF XIAO IF ANYTHING HAPPENED TO ME, AND I BELIEVE HER...
A PROMISE...? HOW CAN SHE PROMISE THAT WHEN SHE DOESN'T EVEN KNOW HOW TO TAKE CARE OF HERSELF?!
TRUST ME: YOU'RE WRONG. YOU WANT A BRIGHT FUTURE FOR XIAO, BUT YOU LEFT WITHOUT HIM...

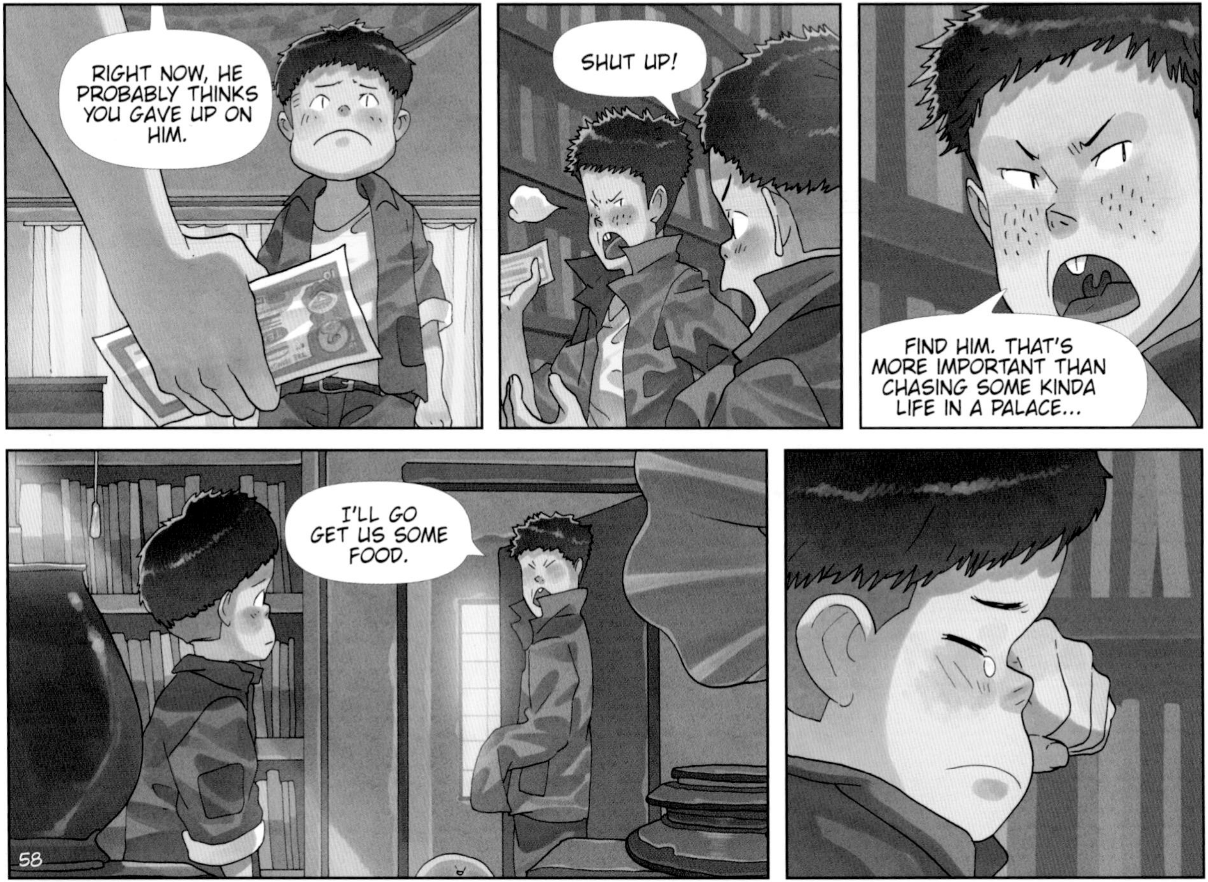
RIGHT NOW, HE PROBABLY THINKS YOU GAVE UP ON HIM.
SHUT UP!
FIND HIM. THAT'S MORE IMPORTANT THAN CHASING SOME KINDA LIFE IN A PALACE...
I'LL GO GET US SOME FOOD.

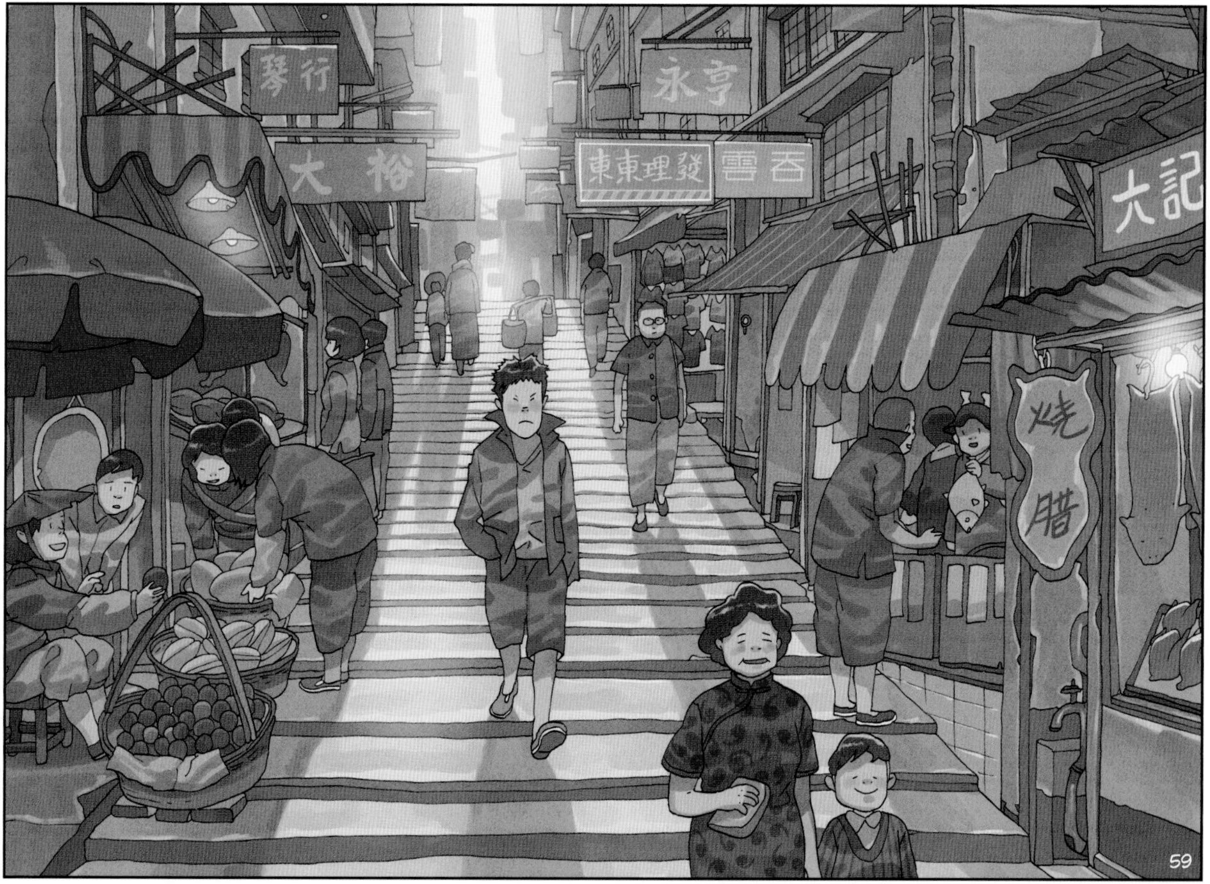
琴行
大裕
永亨
東東理發
大記
烧腊

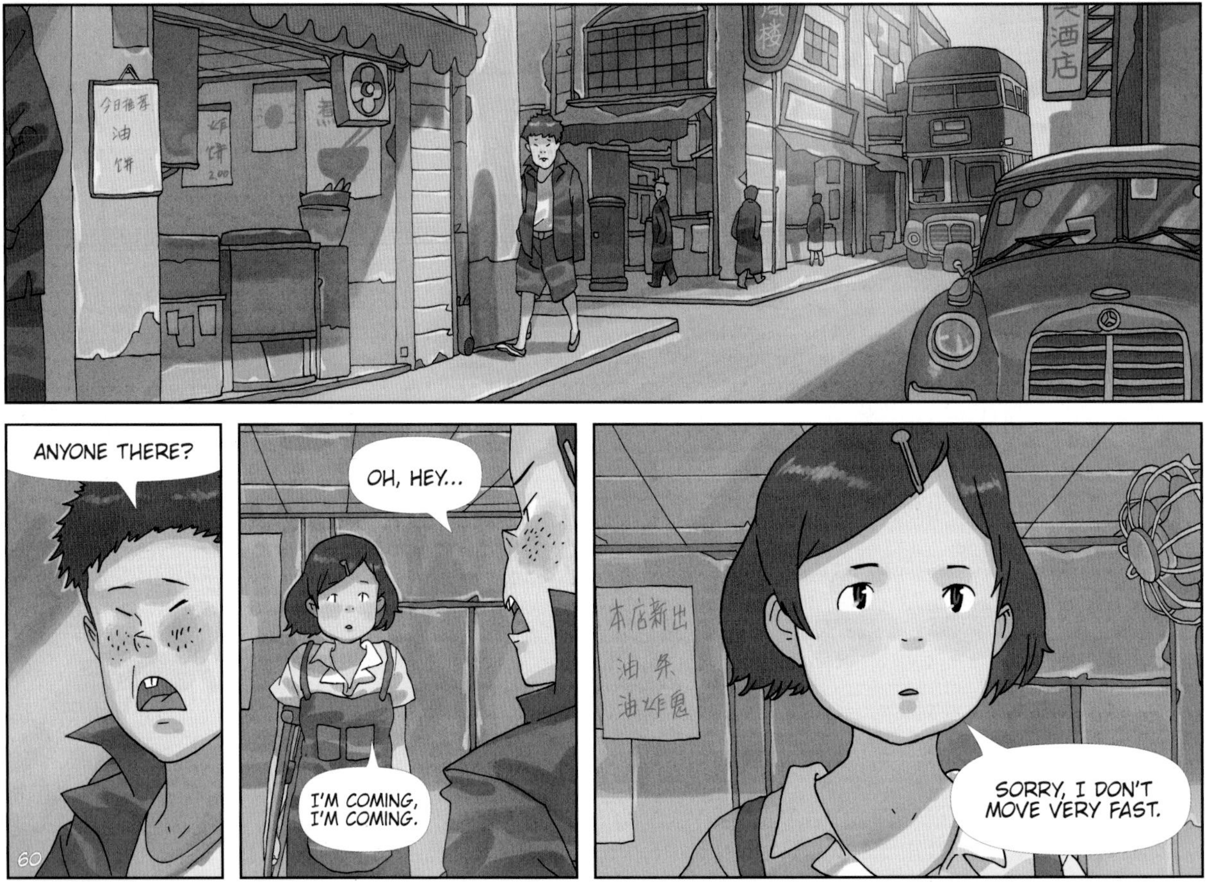
今日推荐
油饼
炸饼
2.00
酒店
ANYONE THERE?
OH, HEY...
I'M COMING, I'M COMING.
本店新出
油条
油炸鬼
SORRY, I DON'T MOVE VERY FAST.

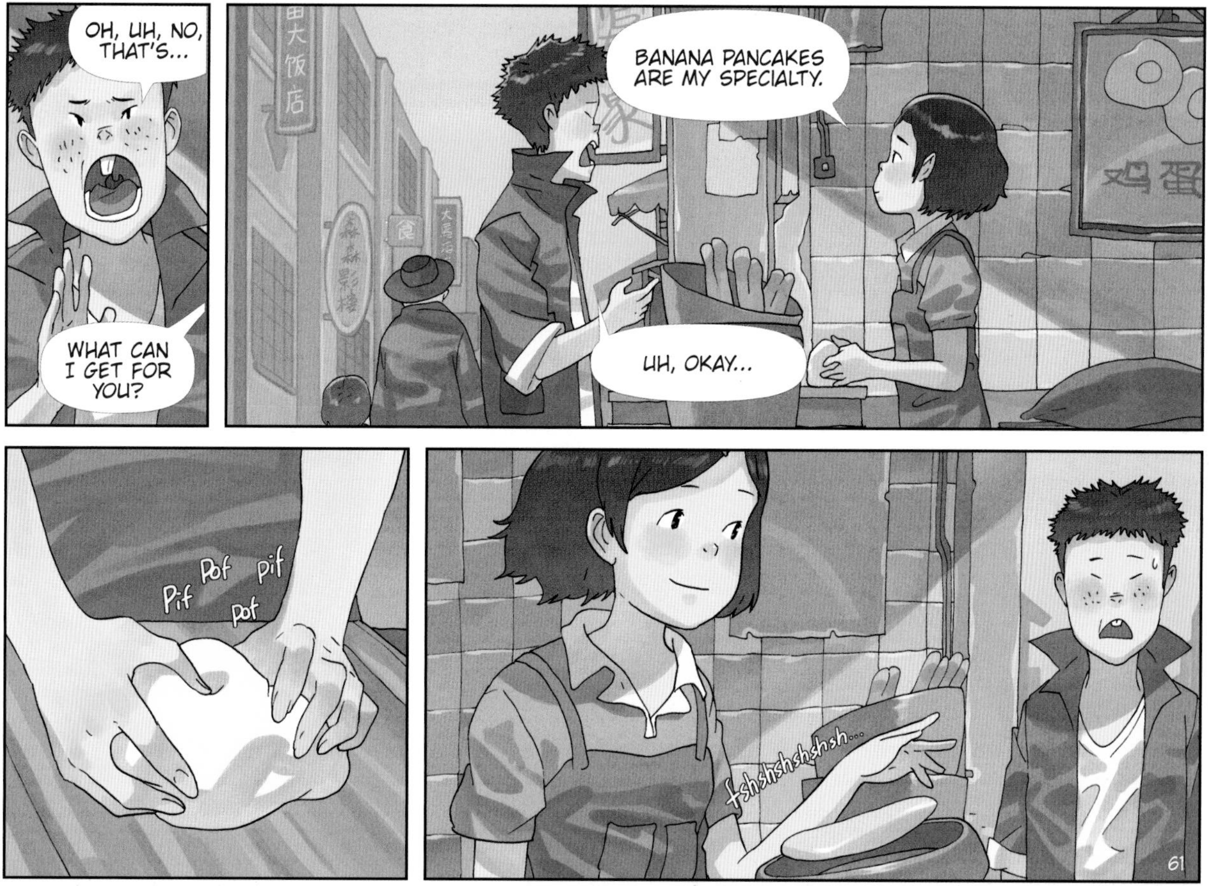
OH, UH, NO, THAT'S...
WHAT CAN I GET FOR YOU?
大饭店
BANANA PANCAKES ARE MY SPECIALTY.
UH, OKAY...
鸡蛋
Pif Pof pif pof
fshshshshshsh...

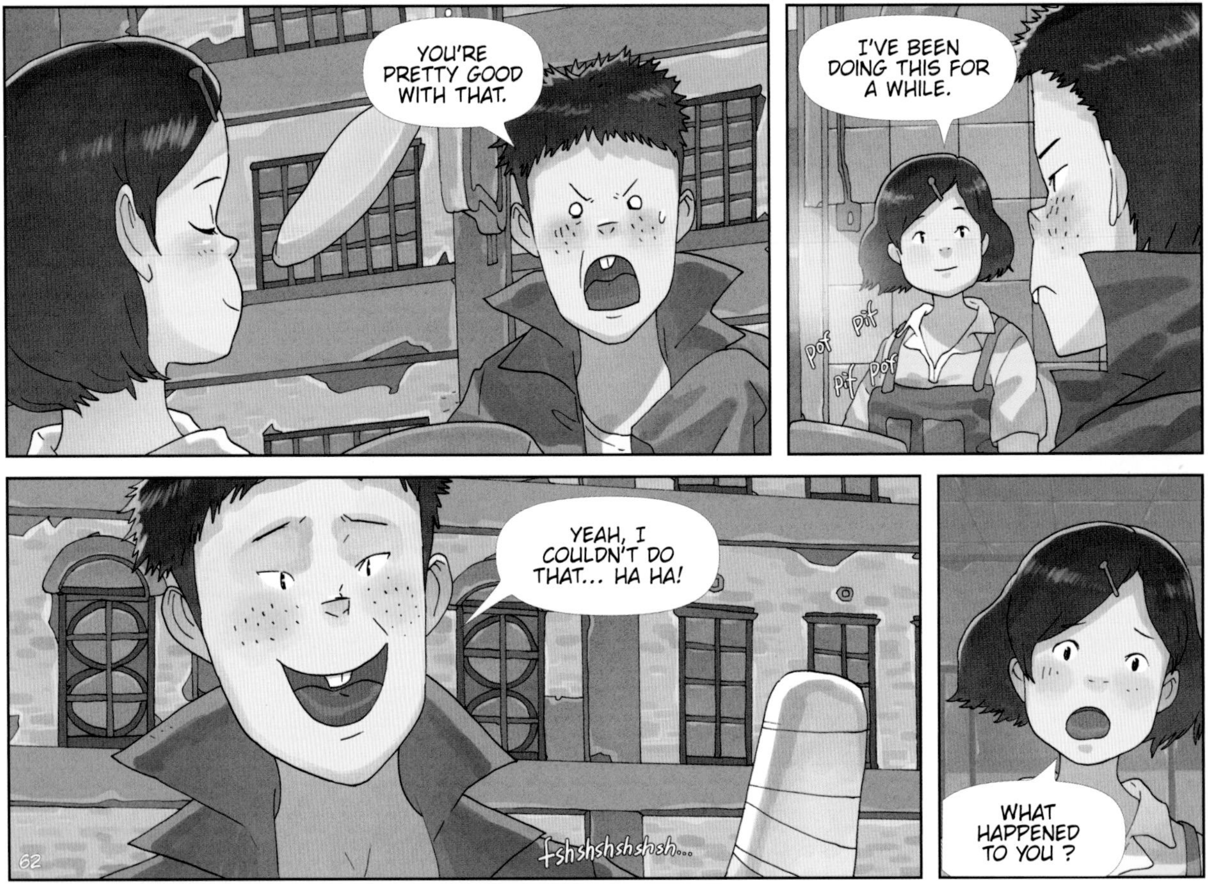
YOU'RE PRETTY GOOD WITH THAT.
I'VE BEEN DOING THIS FOR A WHILE.
pof pif pif pof
YEAH, I COULDN'T DO THAT... HA HA!
fshshshshshsh...
WHAT HAPPENED TO YOU ?

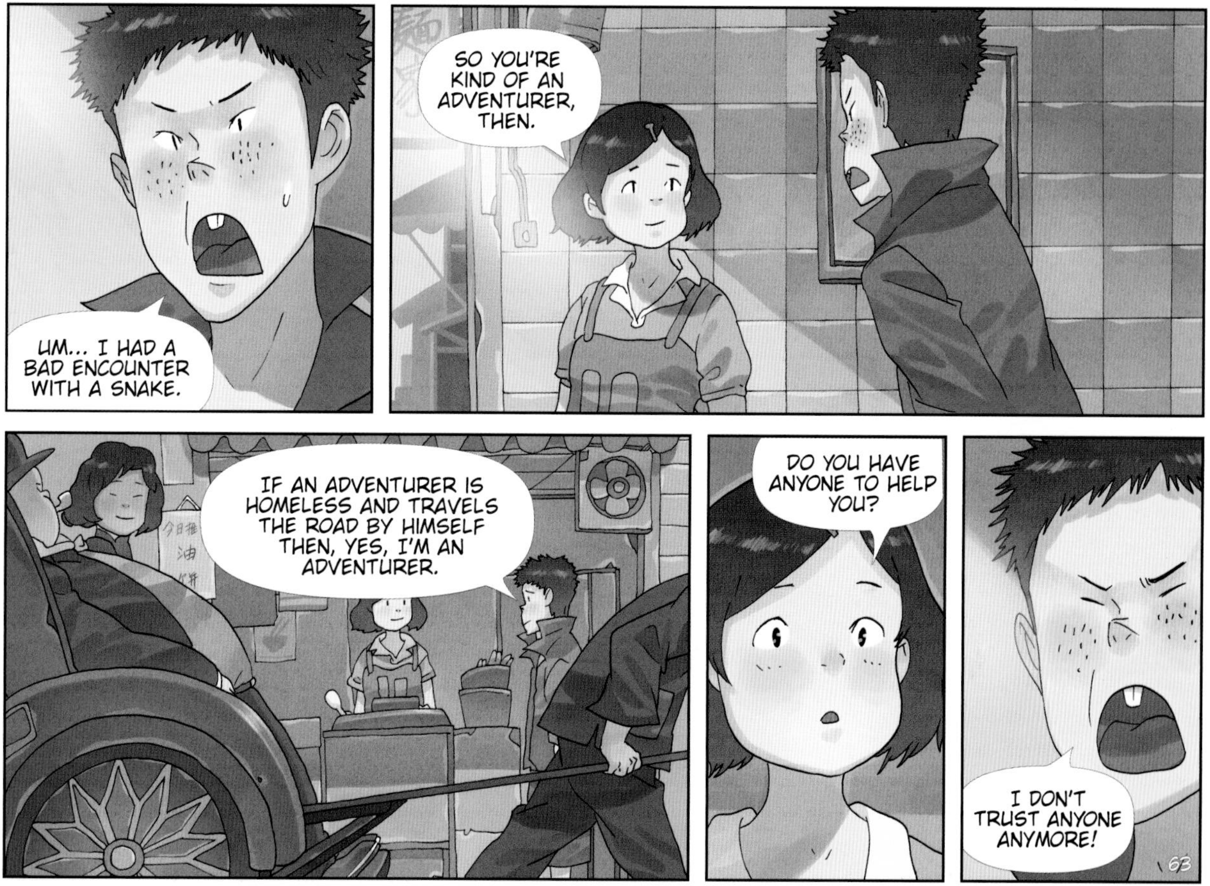
UM... I HAD A BAD ENCOUNTER WITH A SNAKE.
SO YOU'RE KIND OF AN ADVENTURER, THEN.
IF AN ADVENTURER IS HOMELESS AND TRAVELS THE ROAD BY HIMSELF THEN, YES, I'M AN ADVENTURER.
DO YOU HAVE ANYONE TO HELP YOU?
I DON'T TRUST ANYONE ANYMORE!

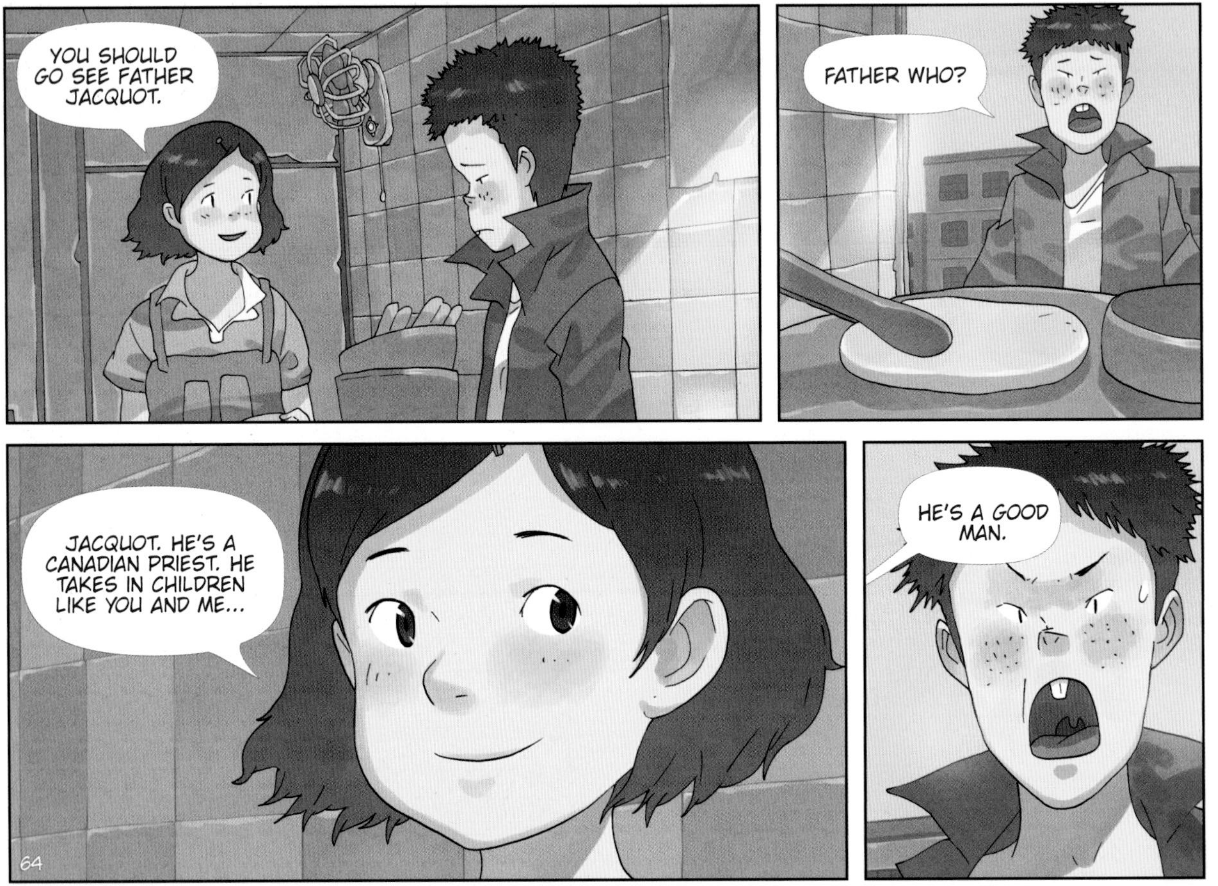
YOU SHOULD GO SEE FATHER JACQUOT.
FATHER WHO?
JACQUOT. HE'S A CANADIAN PRIEST. HE TAKES IN CHILDREN LIKE YOU AND ME...
HE'S A GOOD MAN.

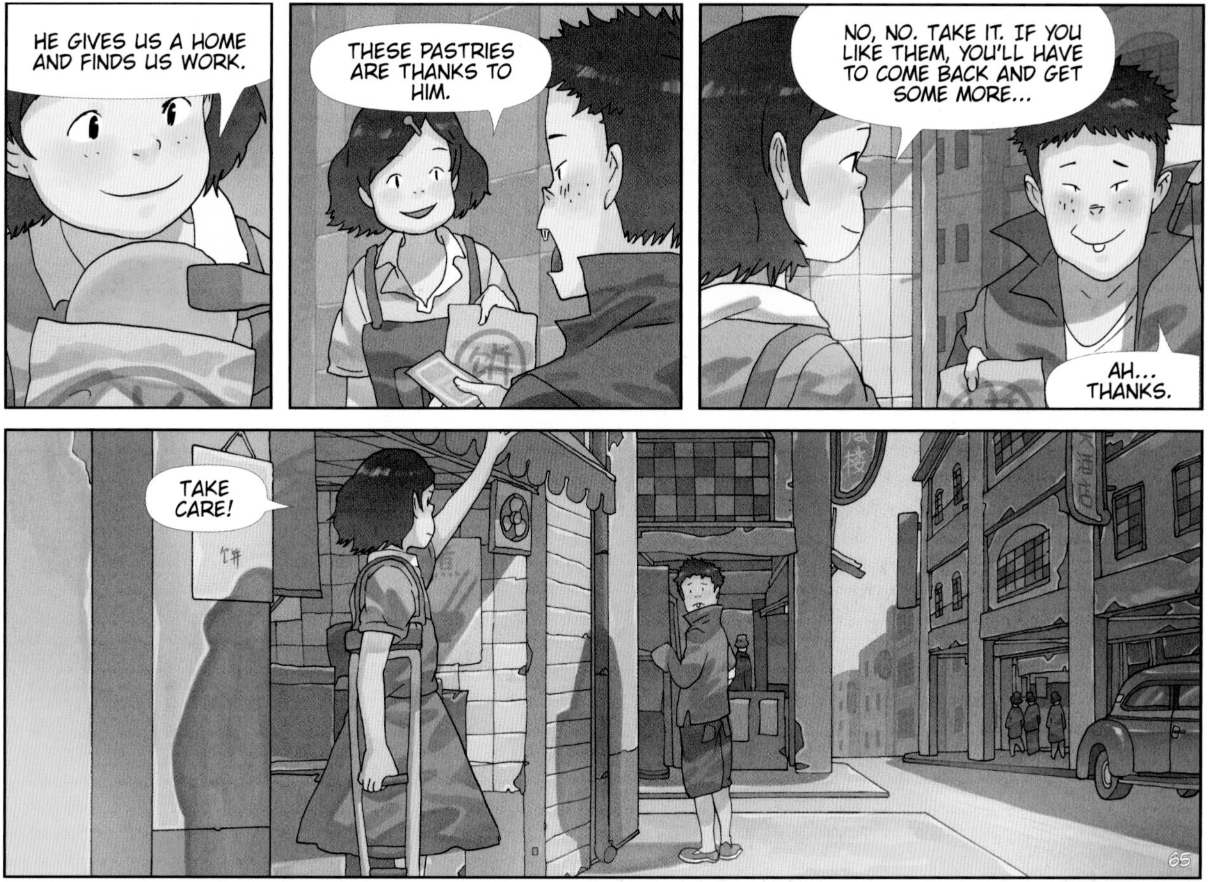
HE GIVES US A HOME AND FINDS US WORK.
THESE PASTRIES ARE THANKS TO HIM.
NO, NO. TAKE IT. IF YOU LIKE THEM, YOU'LL HAVE TO COME BACK AND GET SOME MORE...
AH... THANKS.
TAKE CARE!

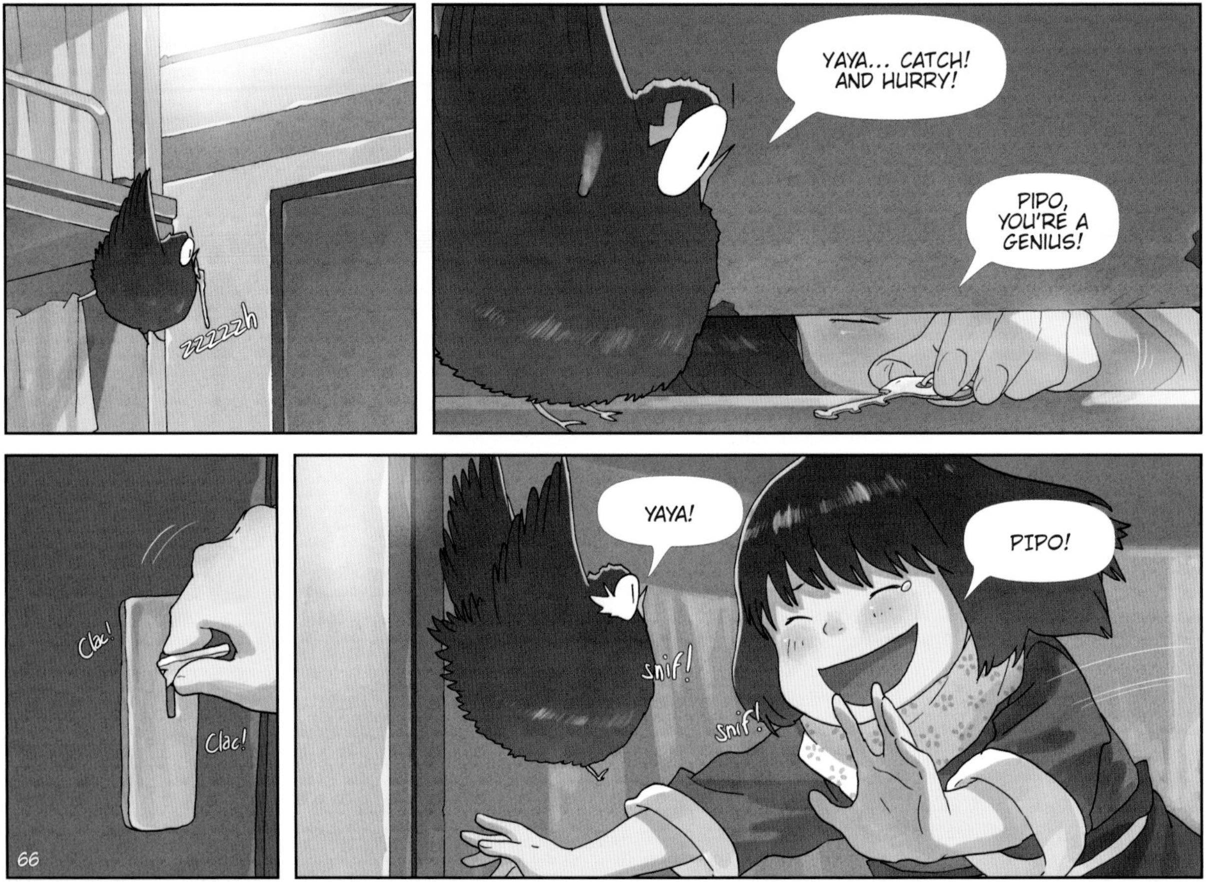
zzzzzh
YAYA... CATCH! AND HURRY!
PIPO, YOU'RE A GENIUS!
Clac!
Clac!
YAYA!
PIPO!
snif!
snif!

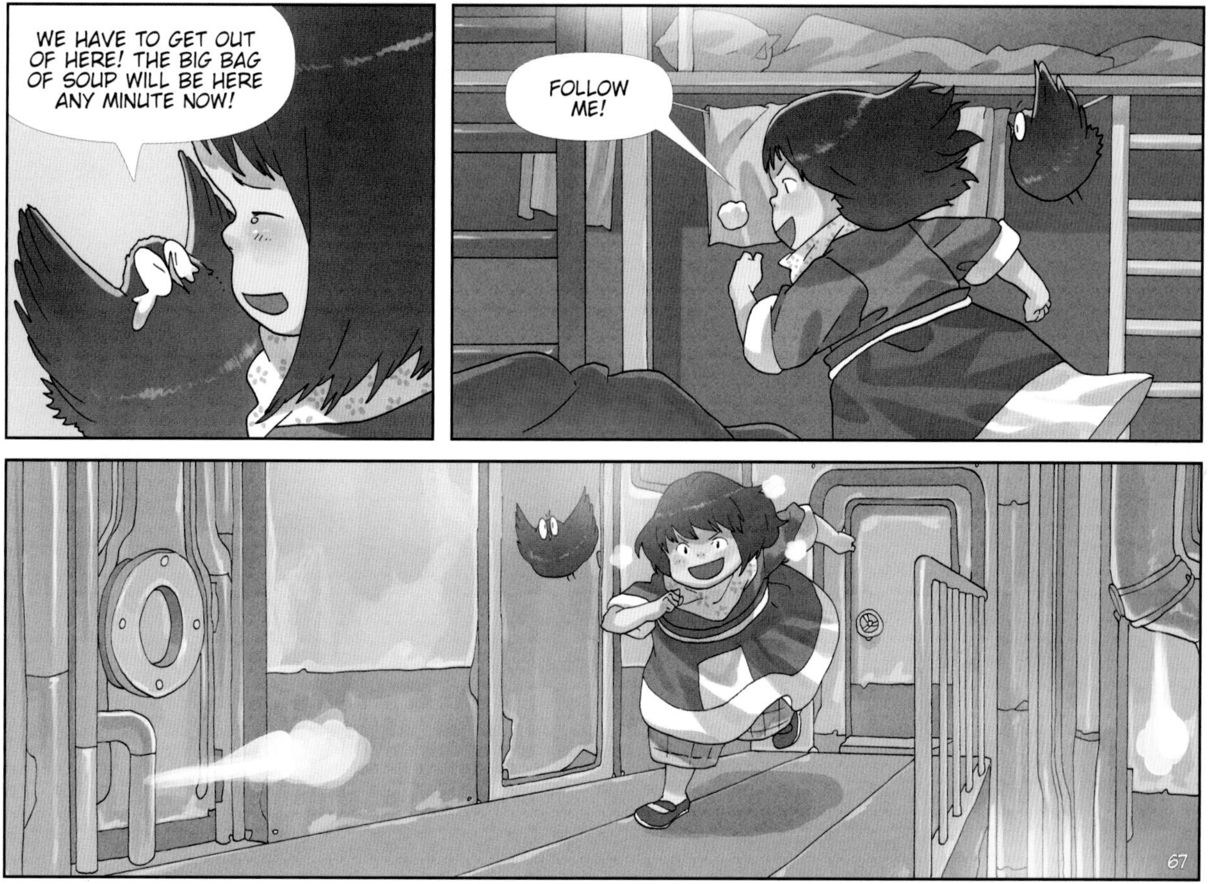
WE HAVE TO GET OUT OF HERE! THE BIG BAG OF SOUP WILL BE HERE ANY MINUTE NOW!
FOLLOW ME!

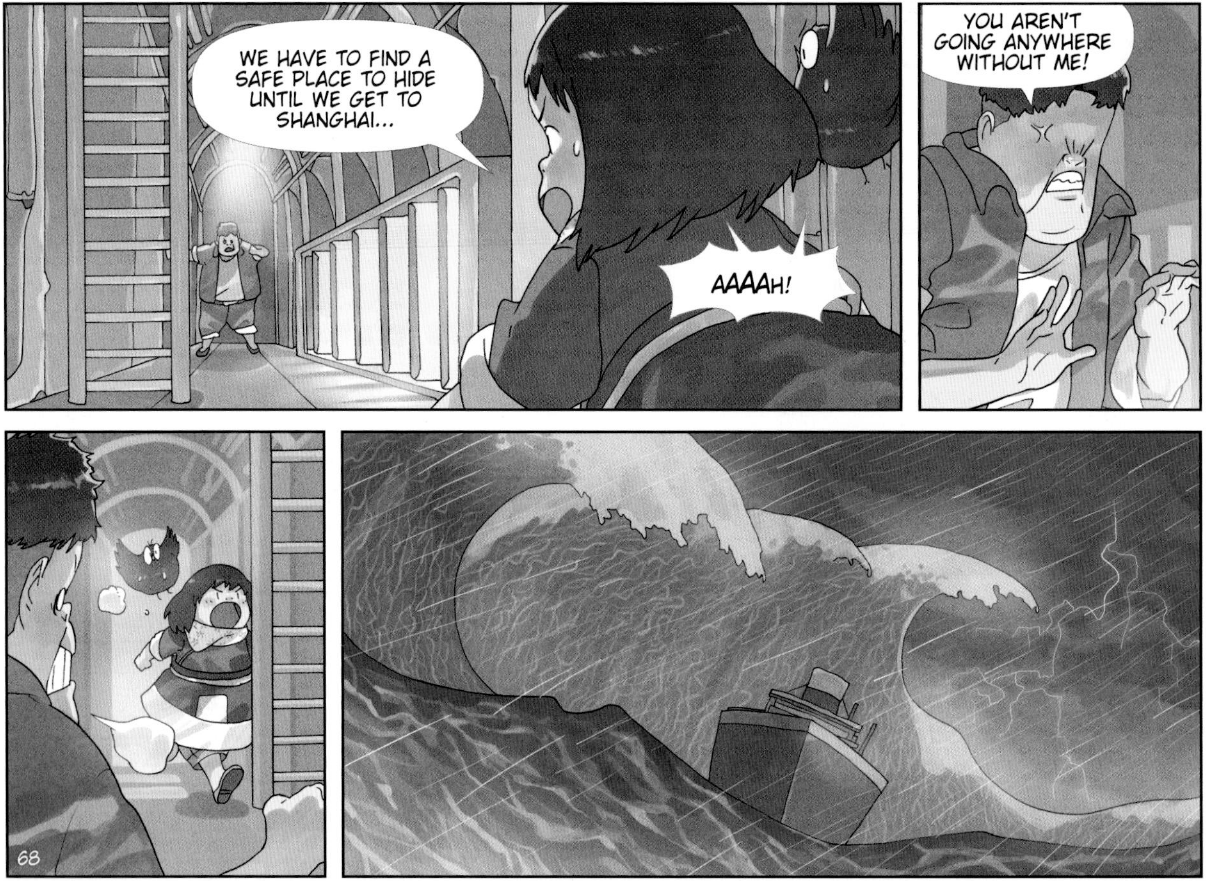
WE HAVE TO FIND A SAFE PLACE TO HIDE UNTIL WE GET TO SHANGHAI...
AAAAH!
YOU AREN'T GOING ANYWHERE WITHOUT ME!

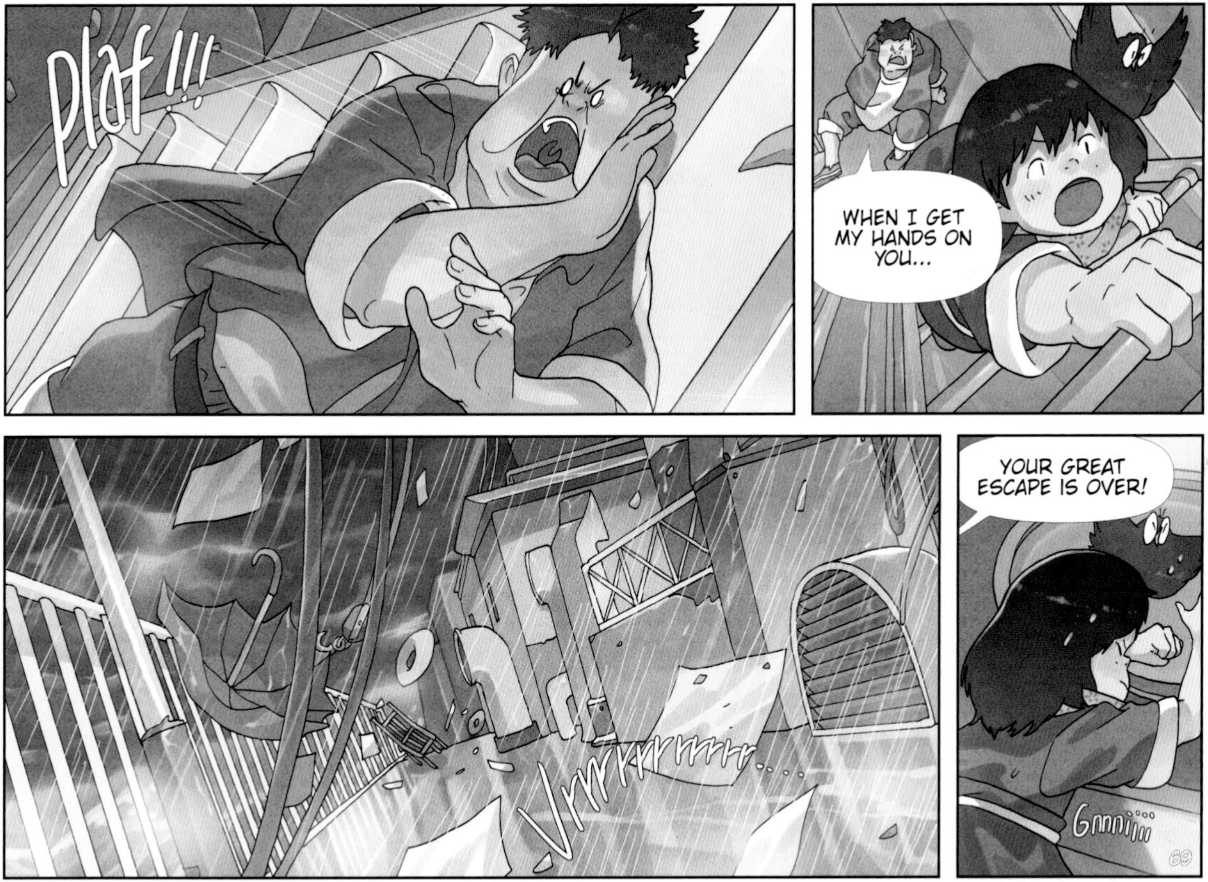
Plaf !!!
WHEN I GET MY HANDS ON YOU...
Vrrrrrrrrrrrrr....
YOUR GREAT ESCAPE IS OVER!
Gnnniiii

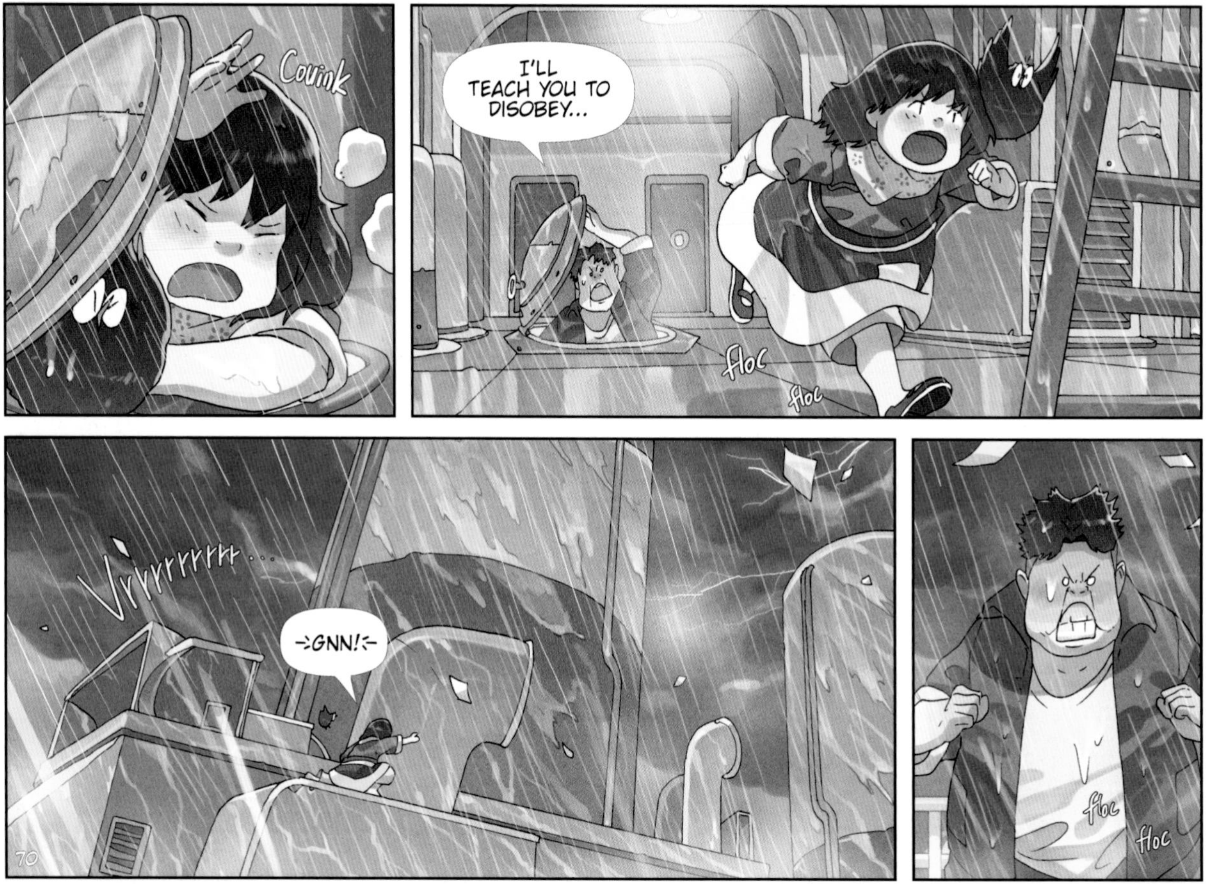
Couink
I'LL TEACH YOU TO DISOBEY...
floc
floc
Vrrrrrrrrr...
-GNN!-
floc
floc

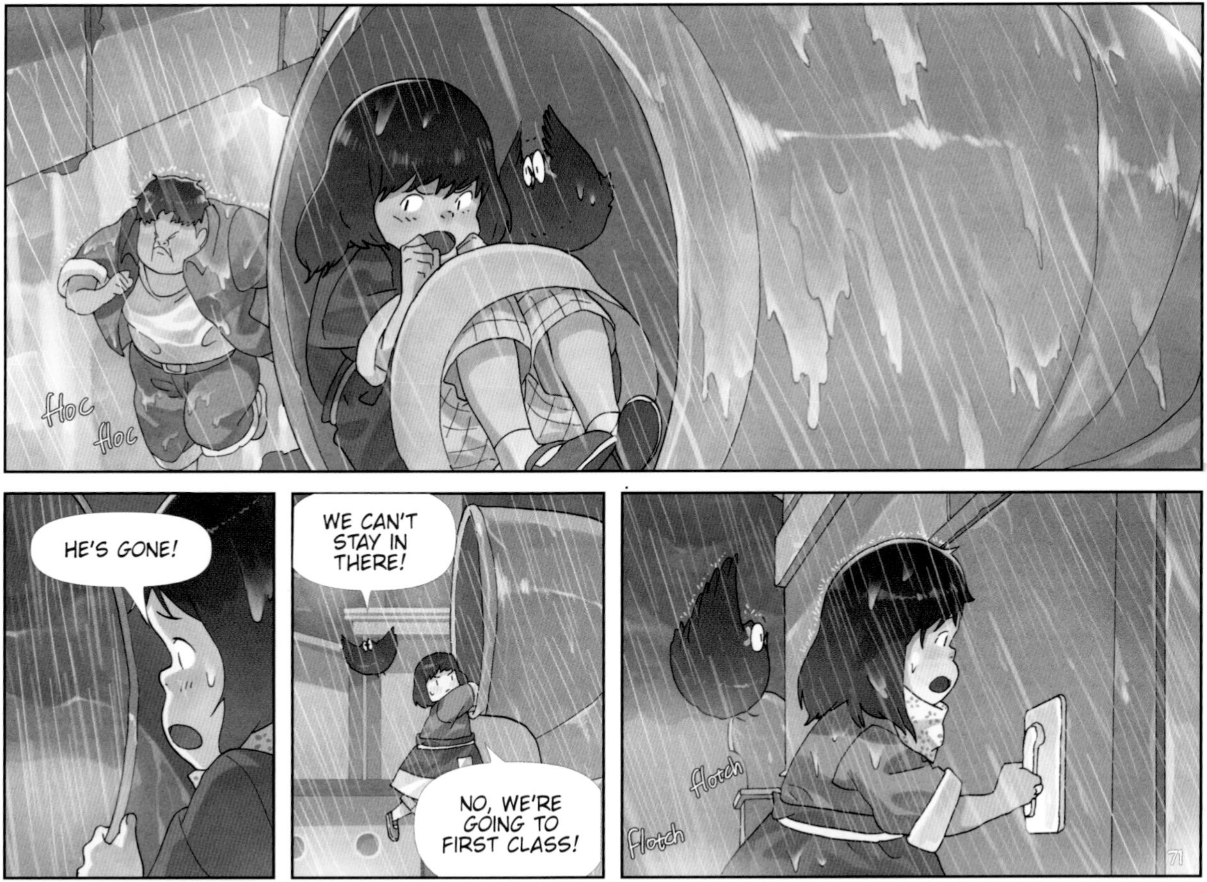
Floc
floc
HE'S GONE!
WE CAN'T STAY IN THERE!
NO, WE'RE GOING TO FIRST CLASS!
flotch
Flotch

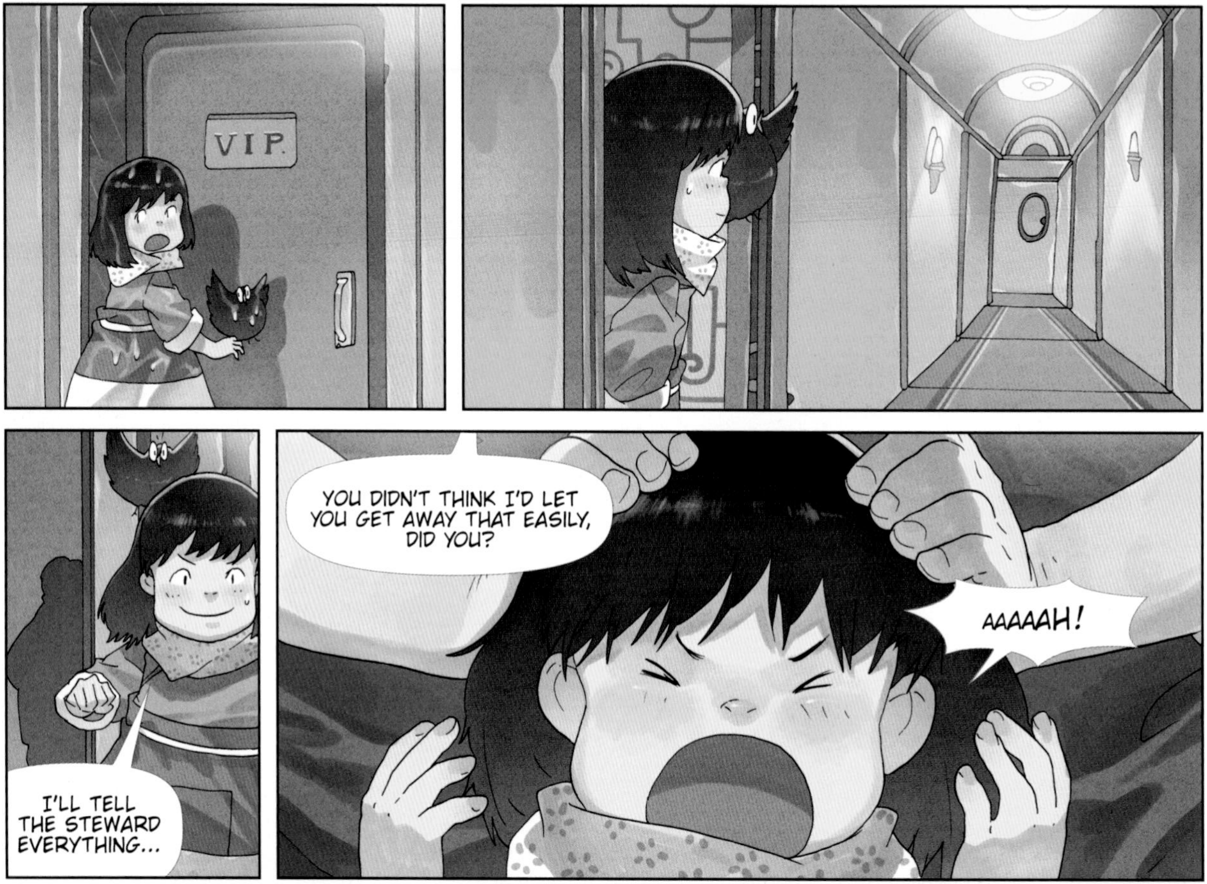
VIP
I'LL TELL THE STEWARD EVERYTHING...
YOU DIDN'T THINK I'D LET YOU GET AWAY THAT EASILY, DID YOU?
AAAAAH!

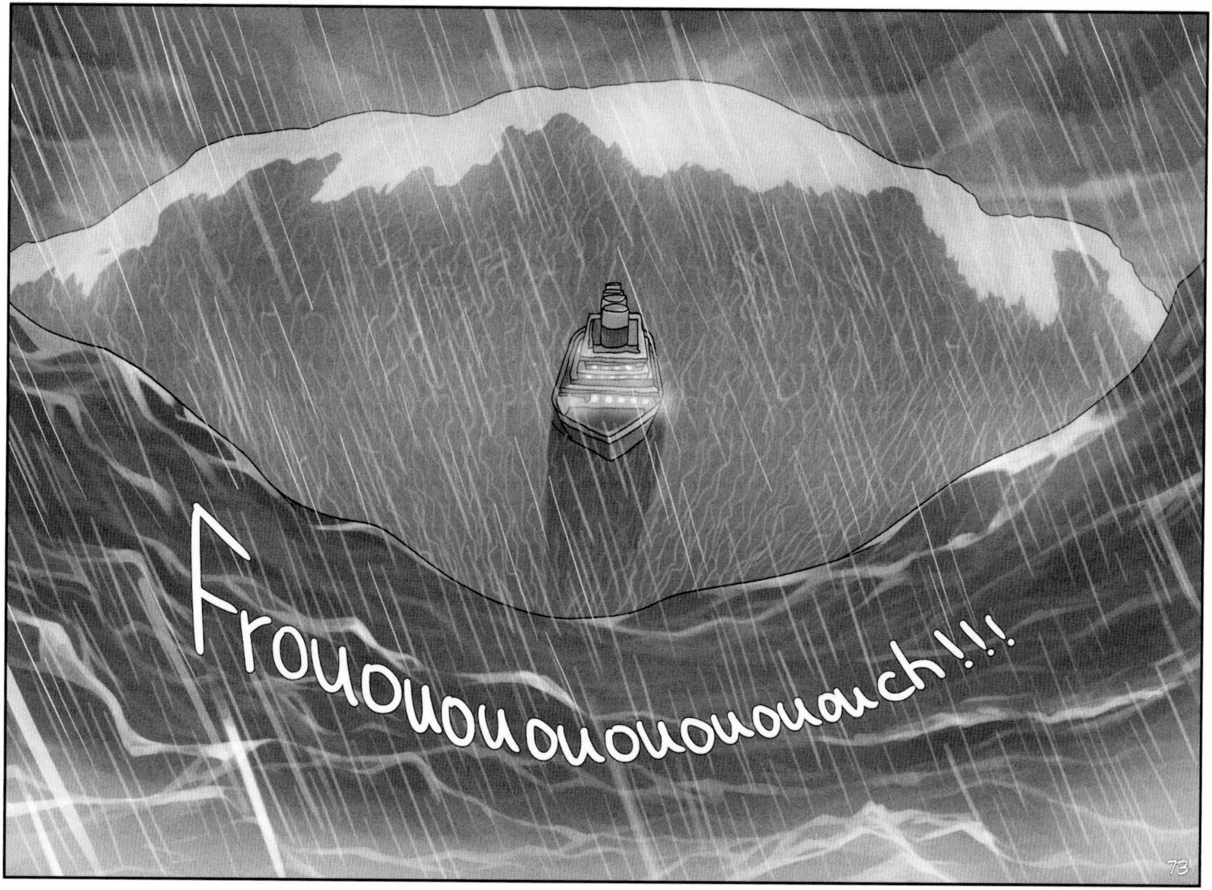
Frououououououououach!!!

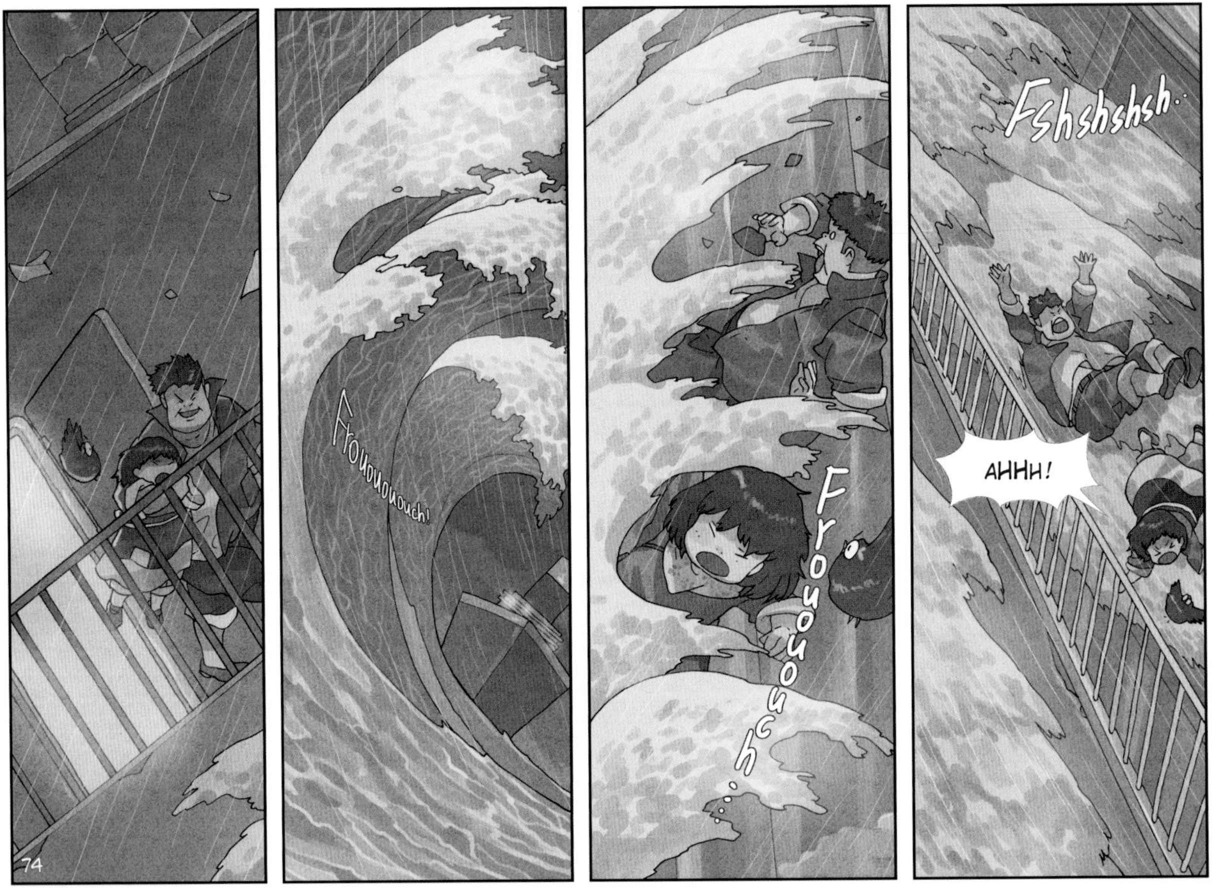
Frououououch!
Frouououch...
Fshshshsh..
AHHH!

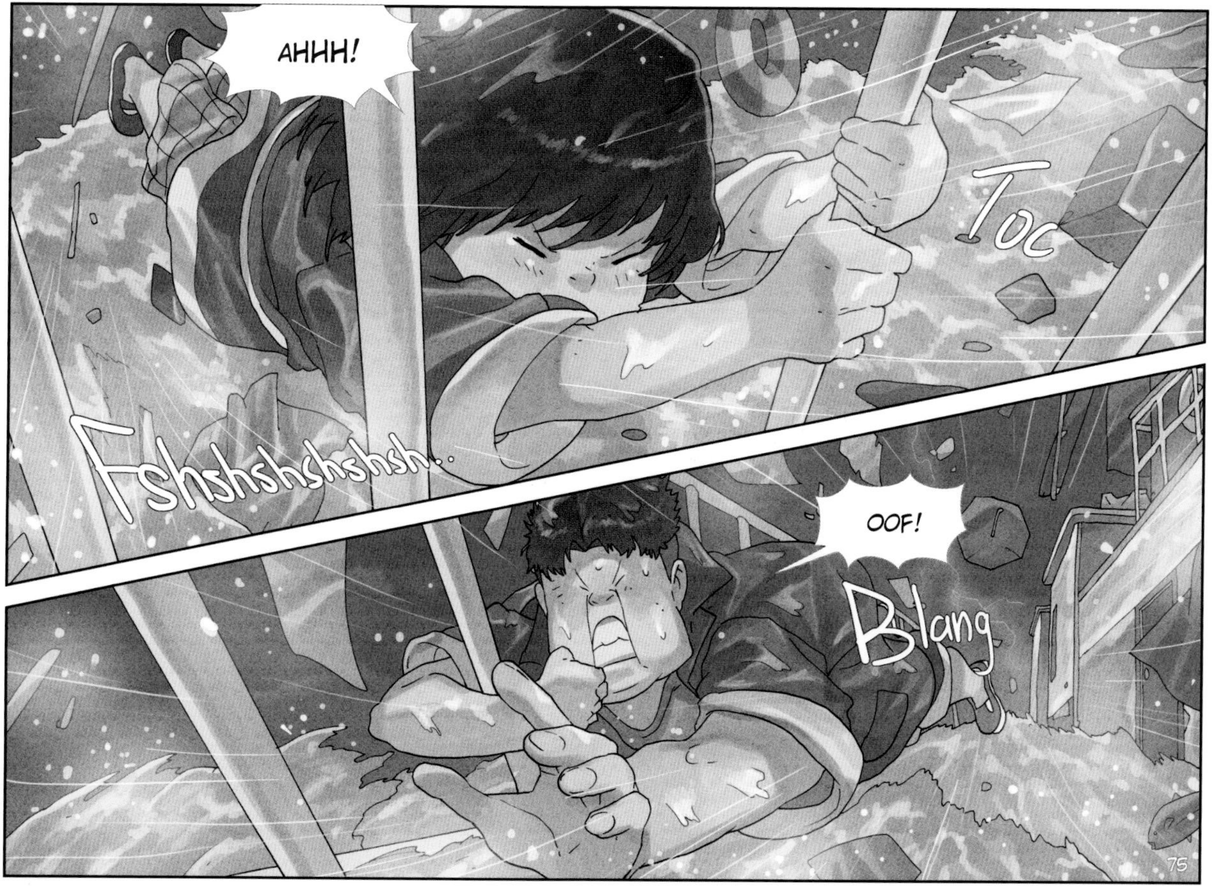
AHHH!
Toc
Fshshshshshsh...
OOF!
Blang

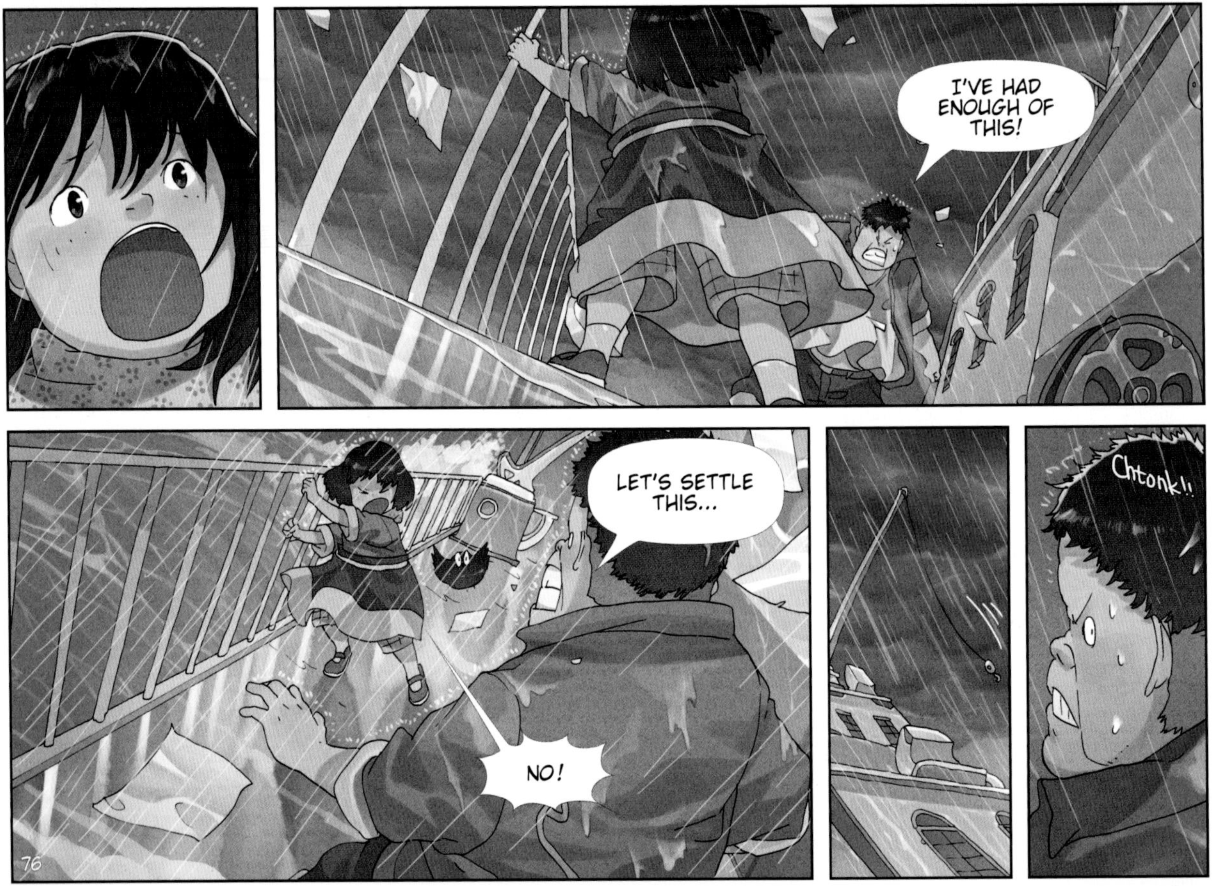
I'VE HAD ENOUGH OF THIS!
LET'S SETTLE THIS...
NO!
Chtonk!!

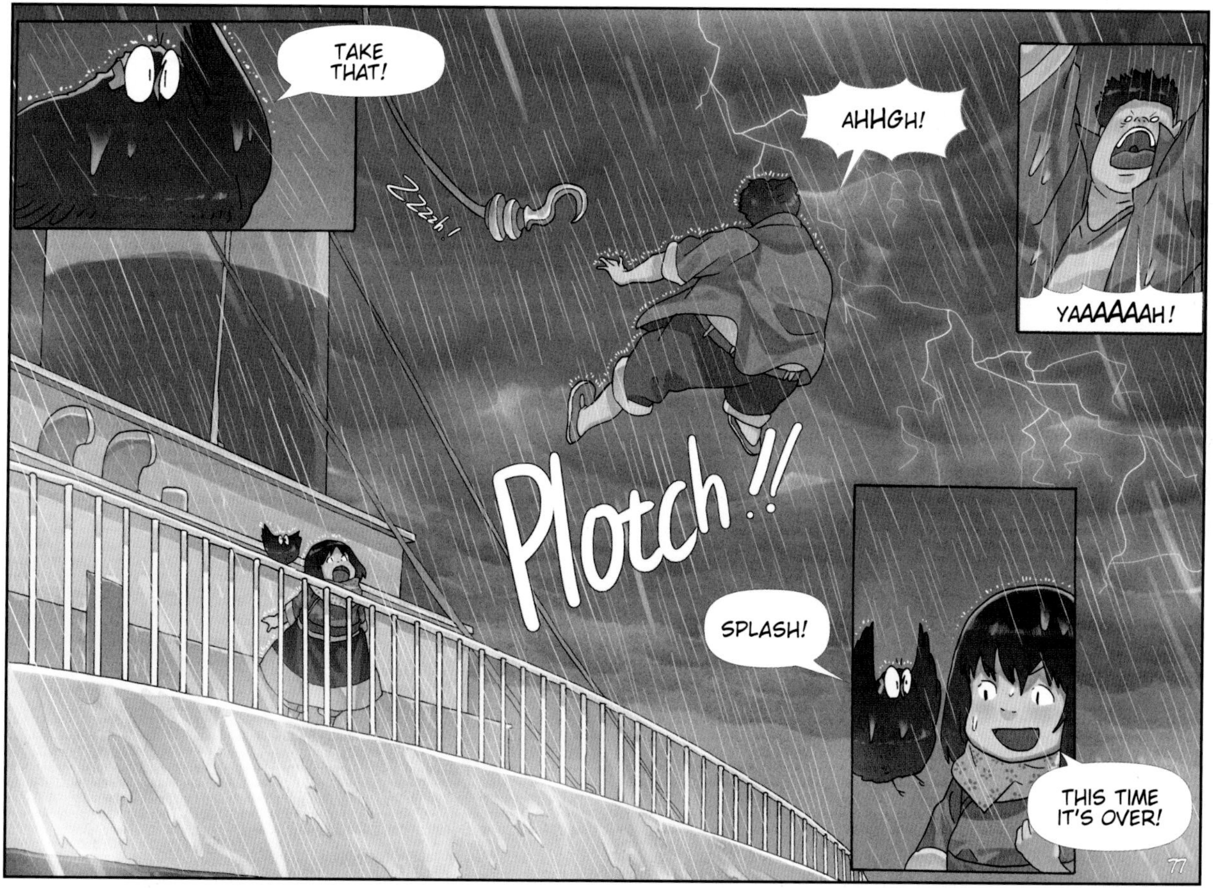
TAKE THAT!
Zzzzh!
AHHGH!
YAAAAAAH!
Plotch!!
SPLASH!
THIS TIME IT'S OVER!

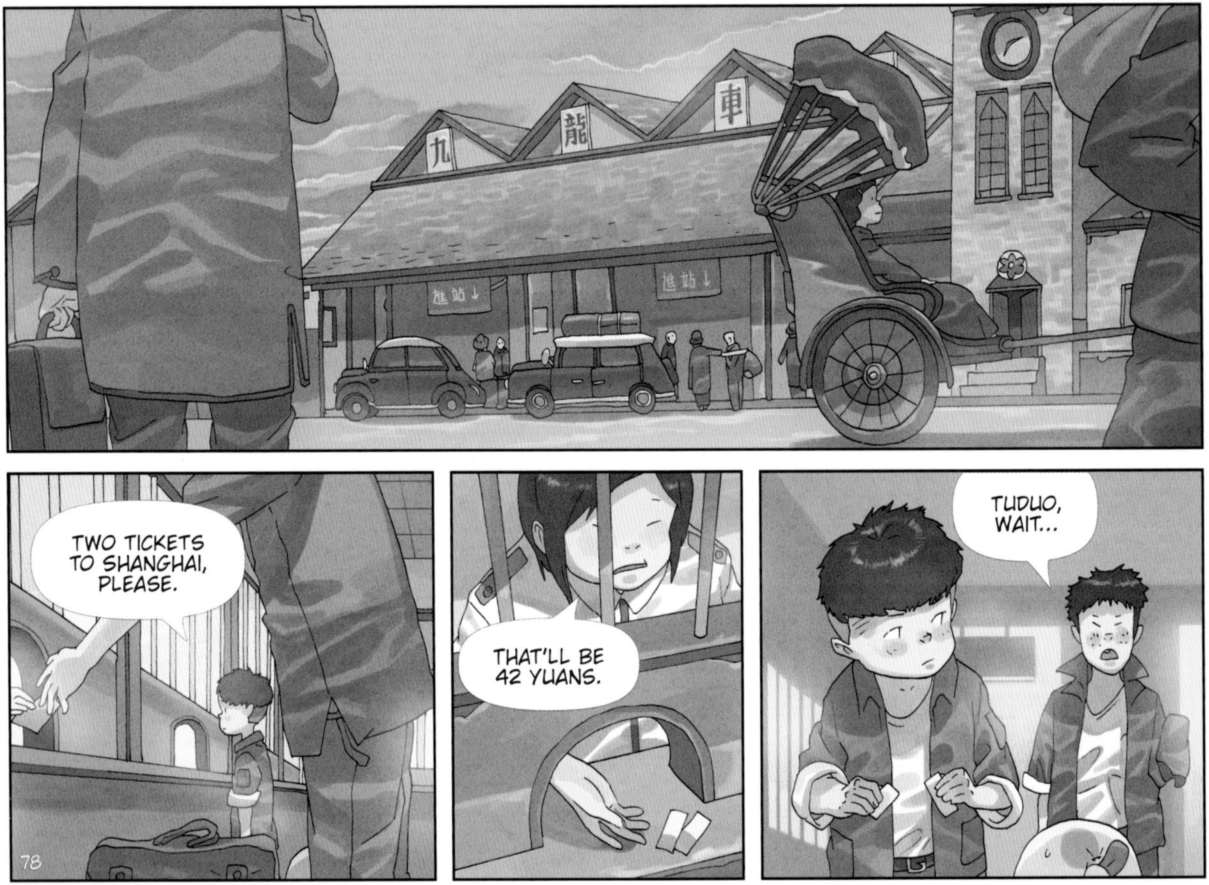
九
龍
車
進站↓
進站↓
TWO TICKETS TO SHANGHAI, PLEASE.
THAT'LL BE 42 YUANS.
TUDUO, WAIT...

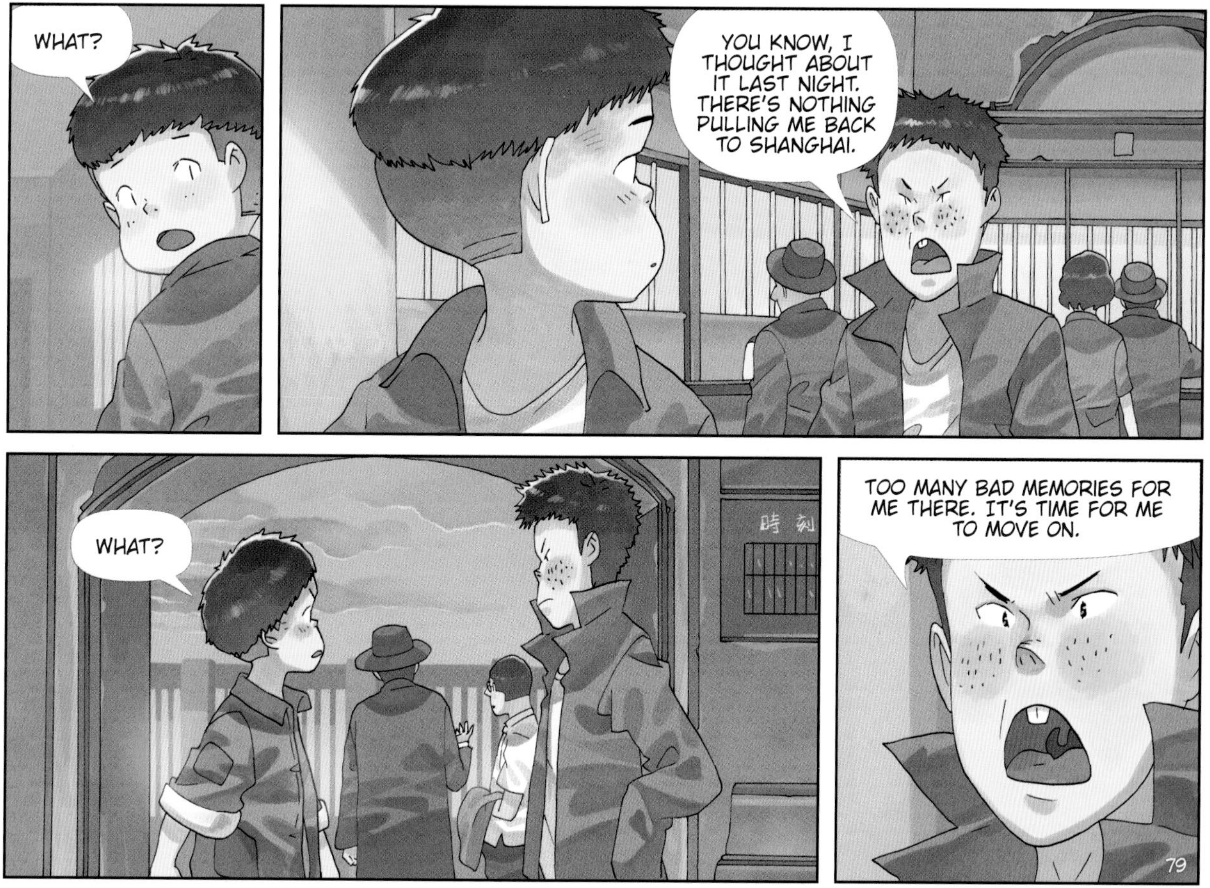
WHAT?
YOU KNOW, I THOUGHT ABOUT IT LAST NIGHT. THERE'S NOTHING PULLING ME BACK TO SHANGHAI.
WHAT?
時刻
TOO MANY BAD MEMORIES FOR ME THERE. IT'S TIME FOR ME TO MOVE ON.

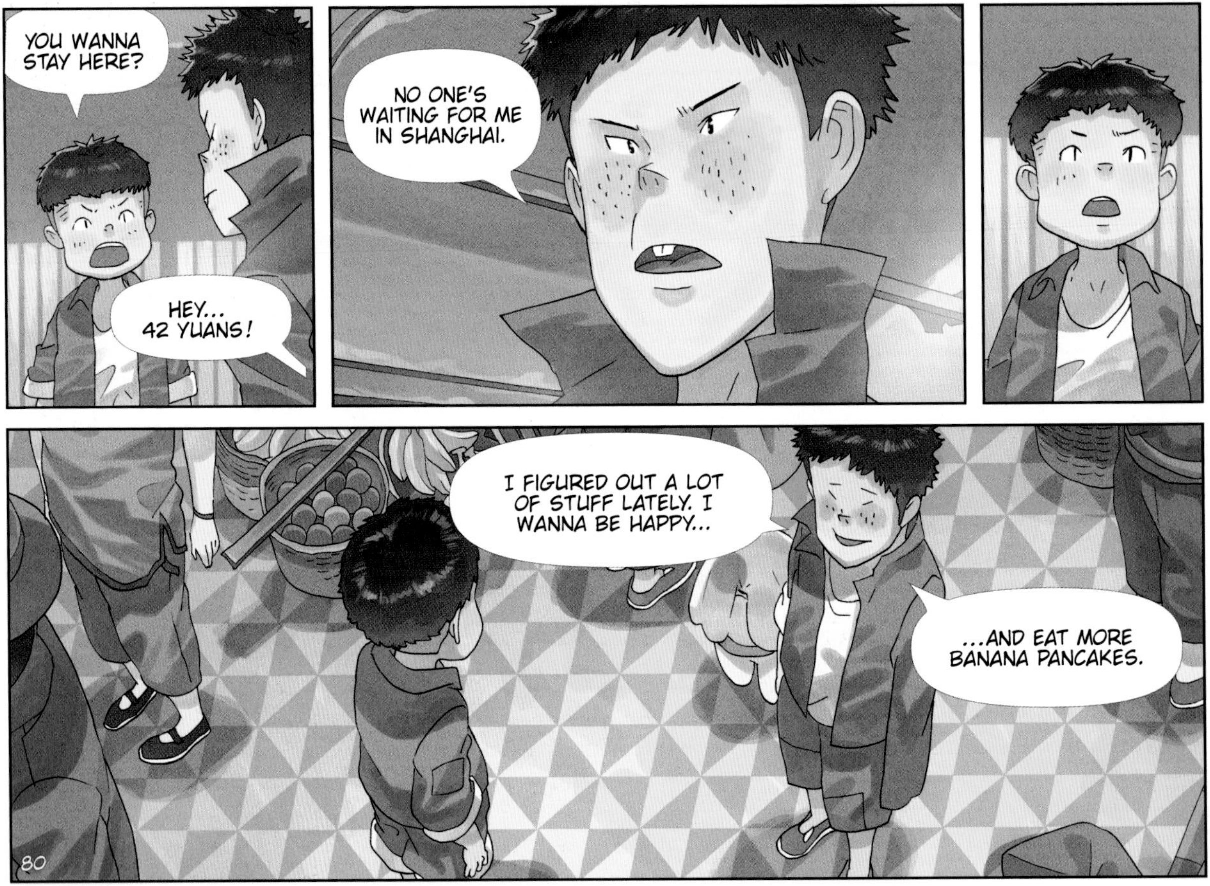
YOU WANNA STAY HERE?
HEY... 42 YUANS!
NO ONE'S WAITING FOR ME IN SHANGHAI.
I FIGURED OUT A LOT OF STUFF LATELY. I WANNA BE HAPPY...
...AND EAT MORE BANANA PANCAKES.

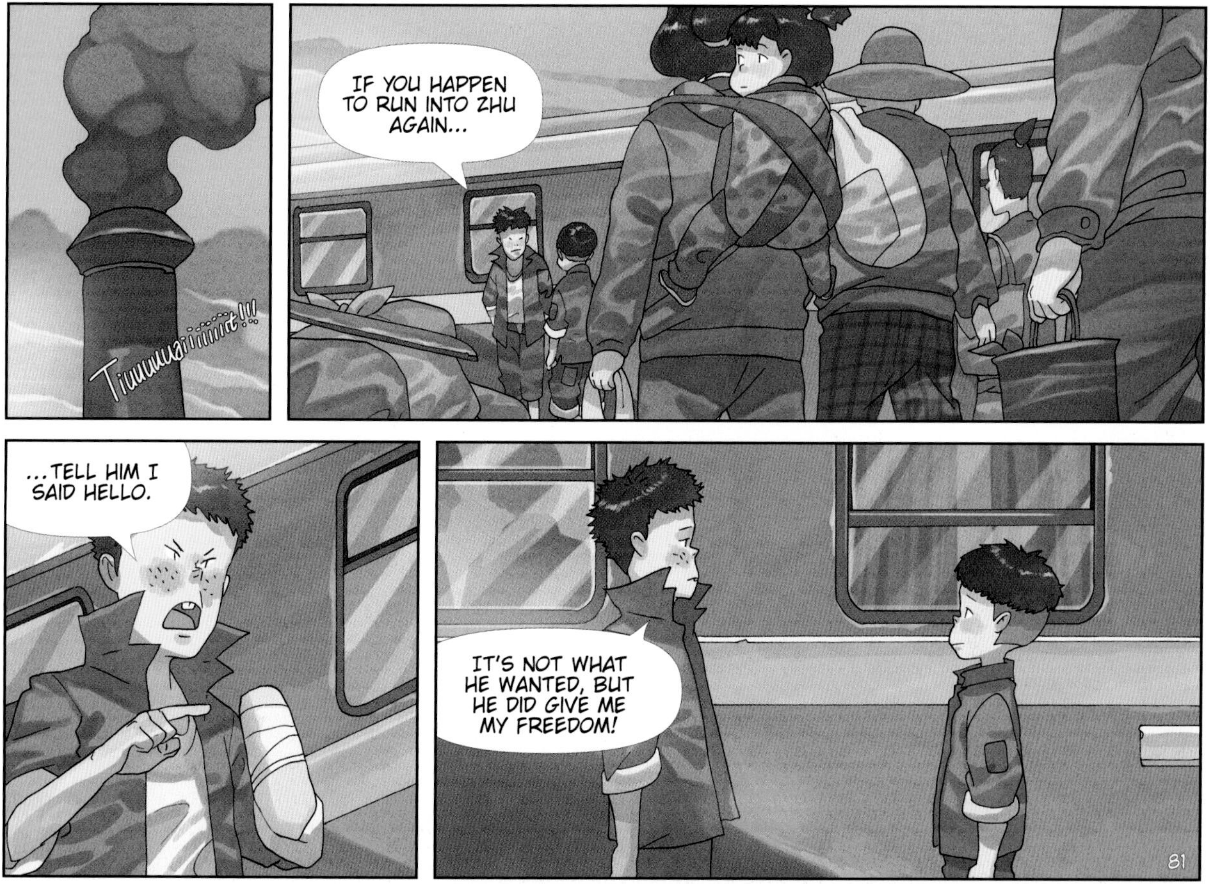
Tiuuuuuaiiiiiiiiiit!!!
IF YOU HAPPEN TO RUN INTO ZHU AGAIN...
...TELL HIM I SAID HELLO.
IT'S NOT WHAT HE WANTED, BUT HE DID GIVE ME MY FREEDOM!

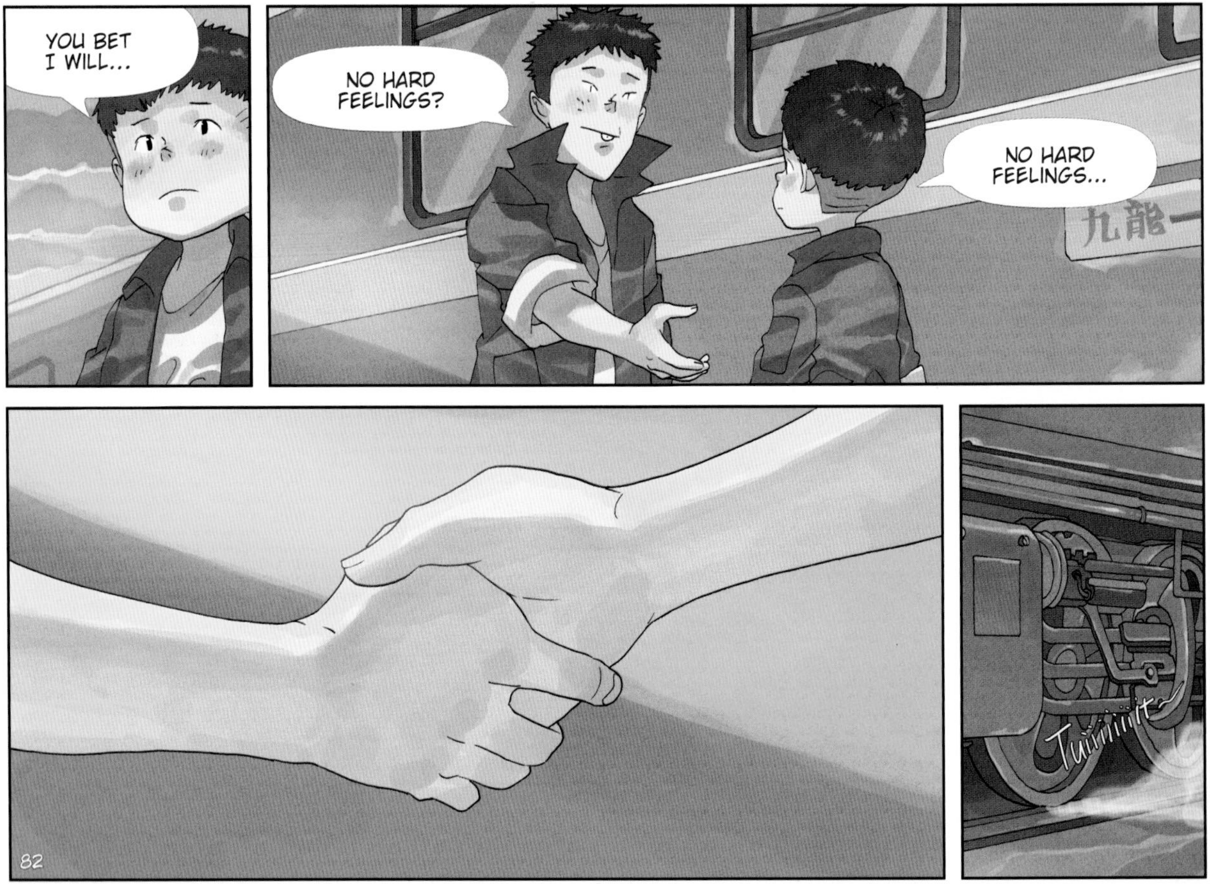
YOU BET I WILL...
NO HARD FEELINGS?
NO HARD FEELINGS...
九龍一
Tuiiiiiiit~

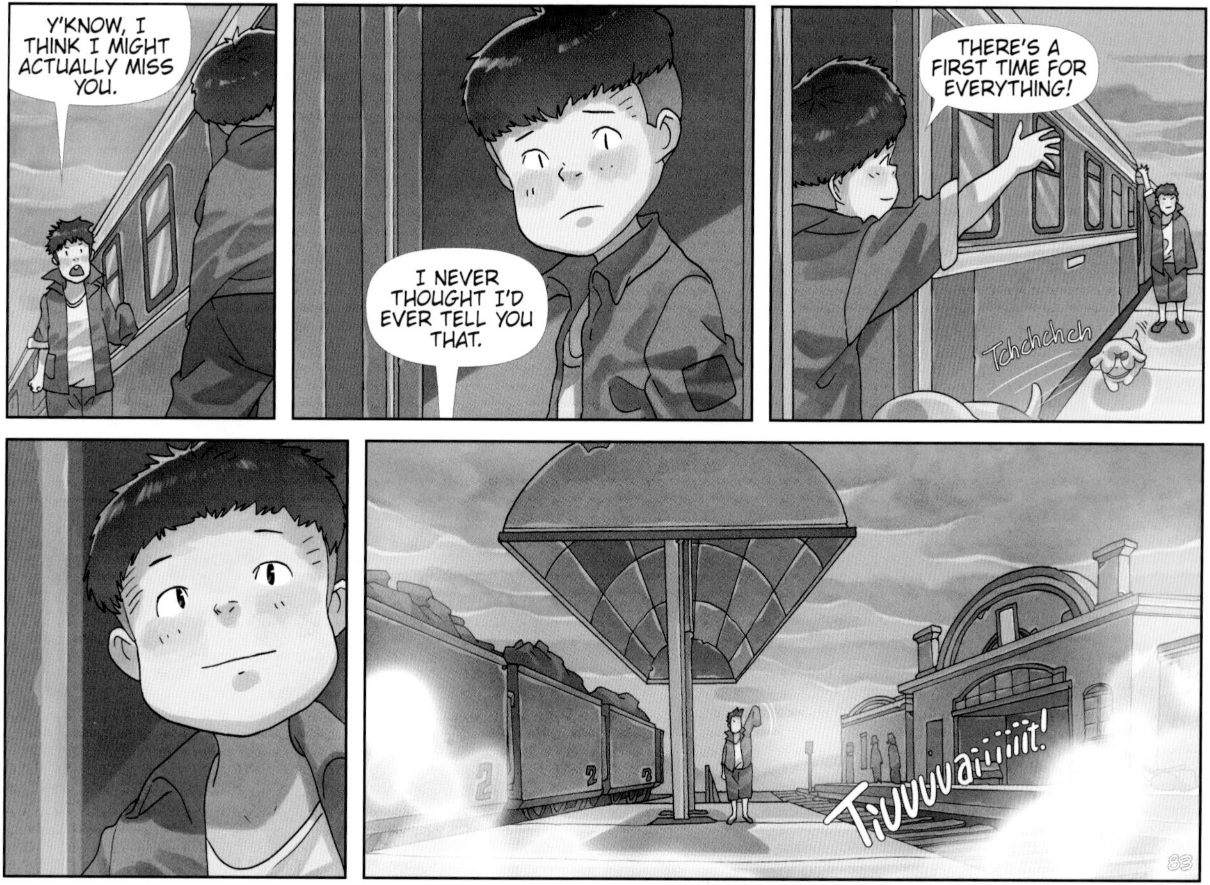
Y'KNOW, I THINK I MIGHT ACTUALLY MISS YOU.
I NEVER THOUGHT I'D EVER TELL YOU THAT.
THERE'S A FIRST TIME FOR EVERYTHING!
Tchchchch
Tiuuuuaiiiiiit!

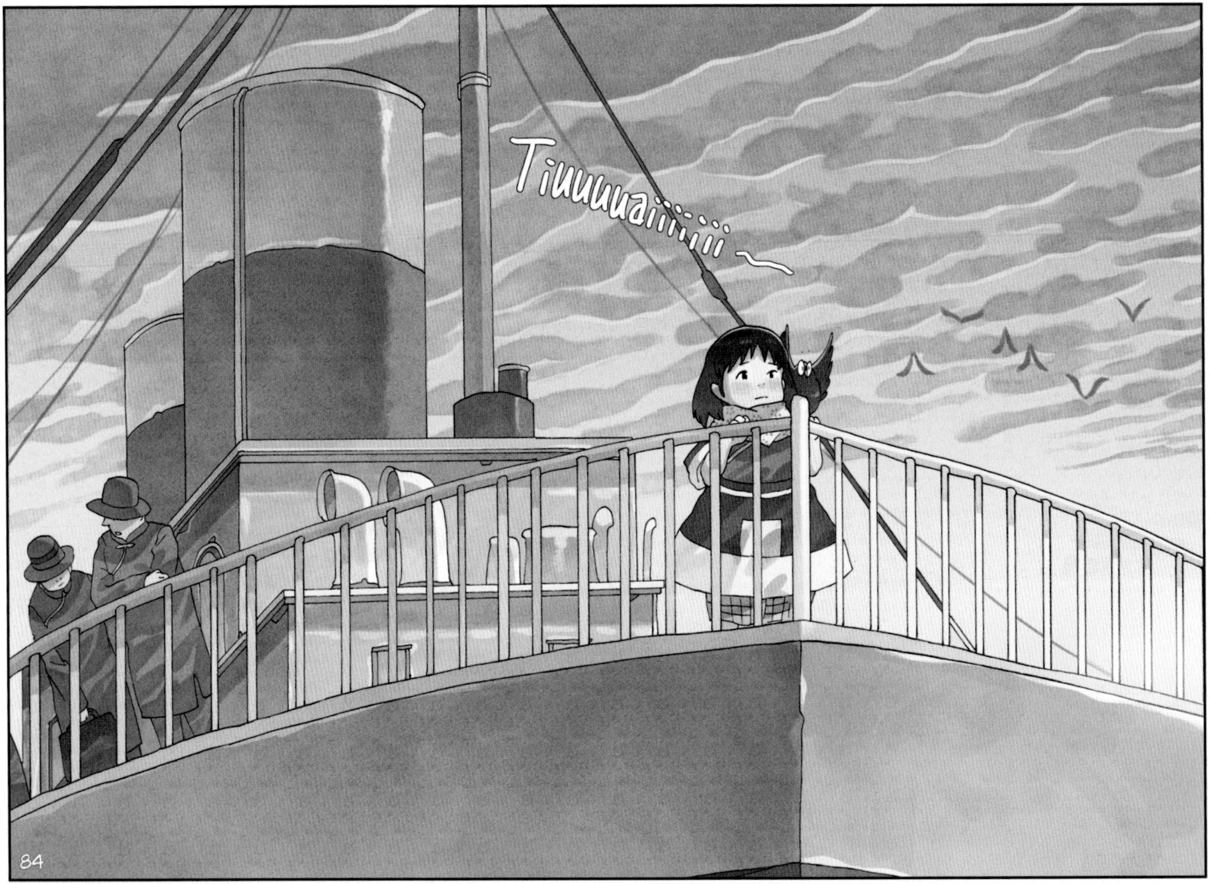
Tiuuuuaiiiiiiii~

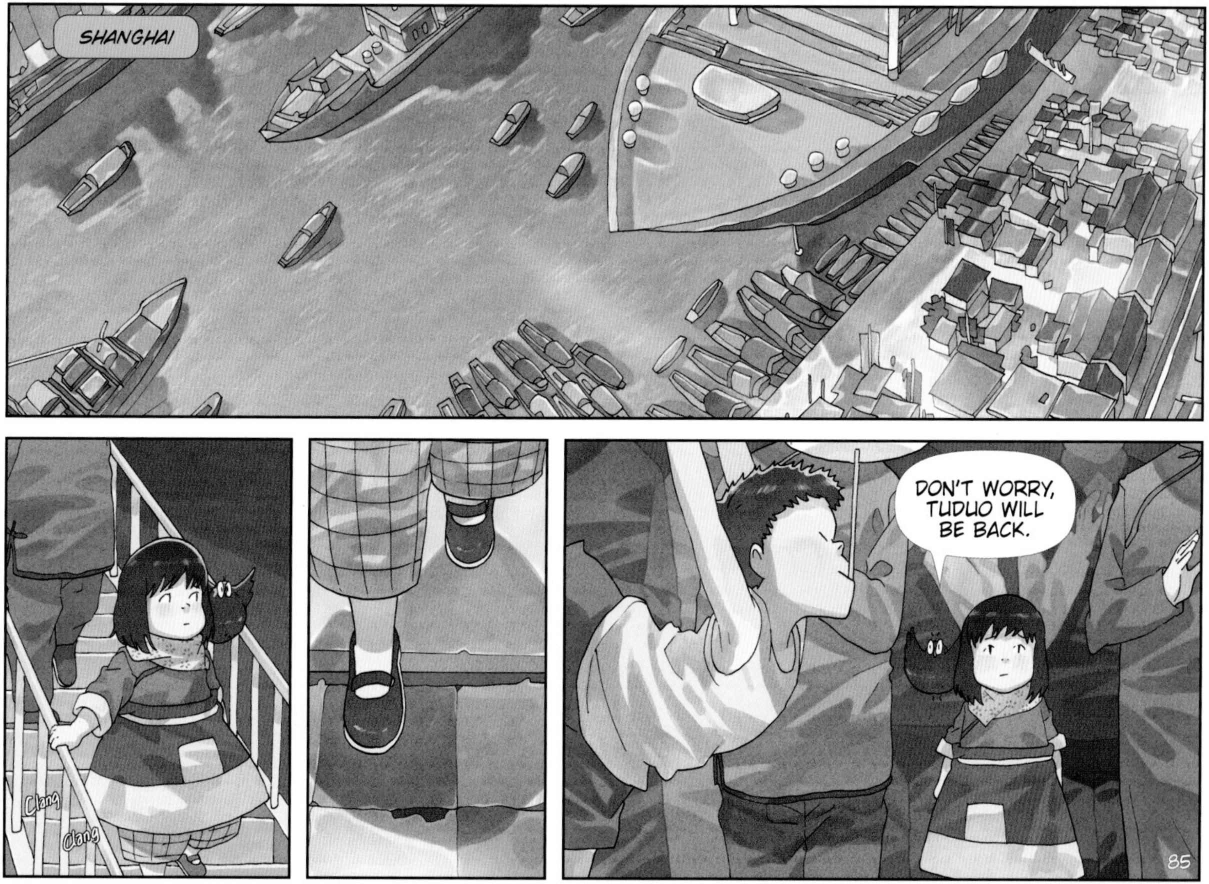
SHANGHAI
Clang
Clang
DON'T WORRY, TUDUO WILL BE BACK.

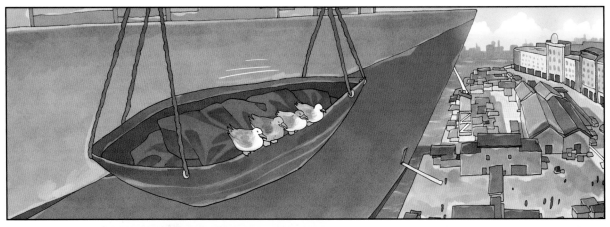

~ARGH!~
WHAT IS
THIS...?

Clop!

HMMMHHH?

OH NO, MY
LITTLE ONE... YOU
HAVEN'T GOTTEN
RID OF ME YET!

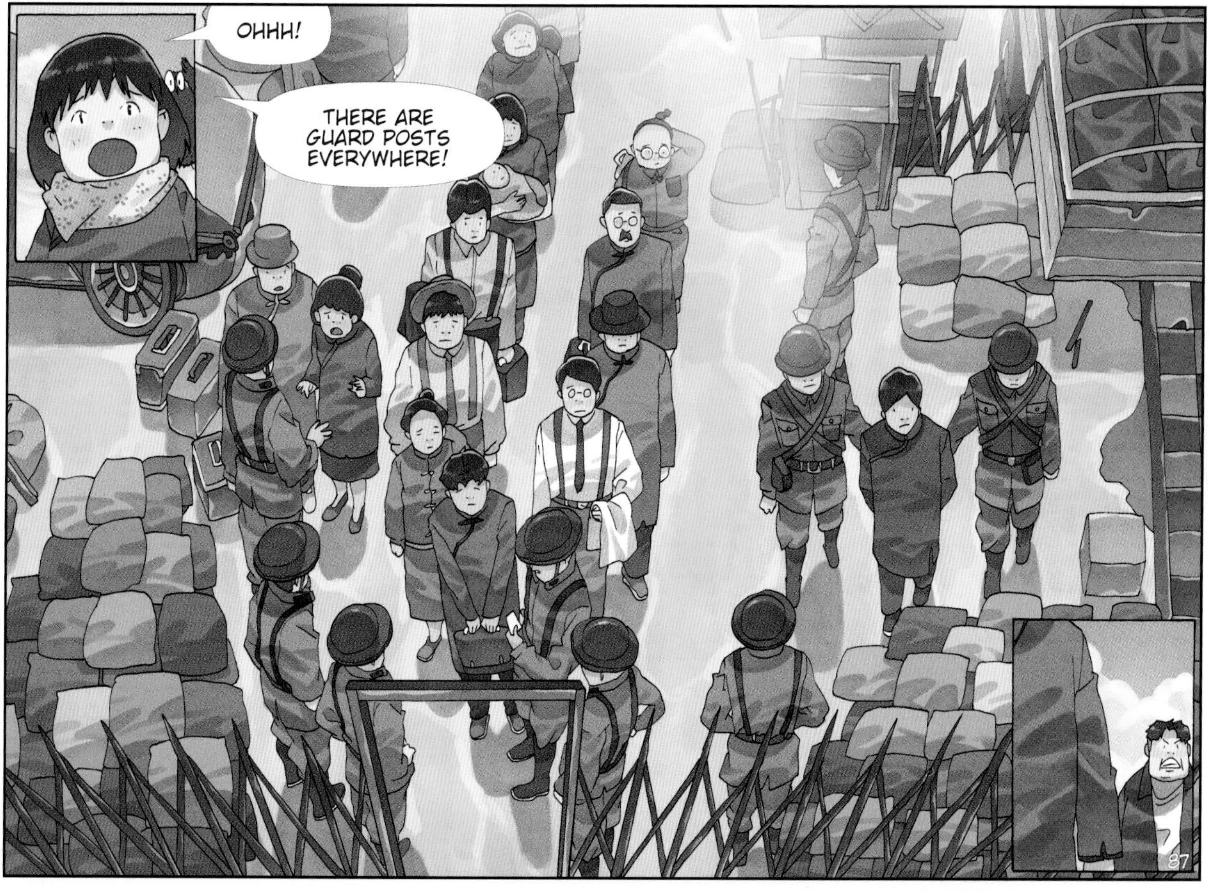
OHHH!
THERE ARE GUARD POSTS EVERYWHERE!

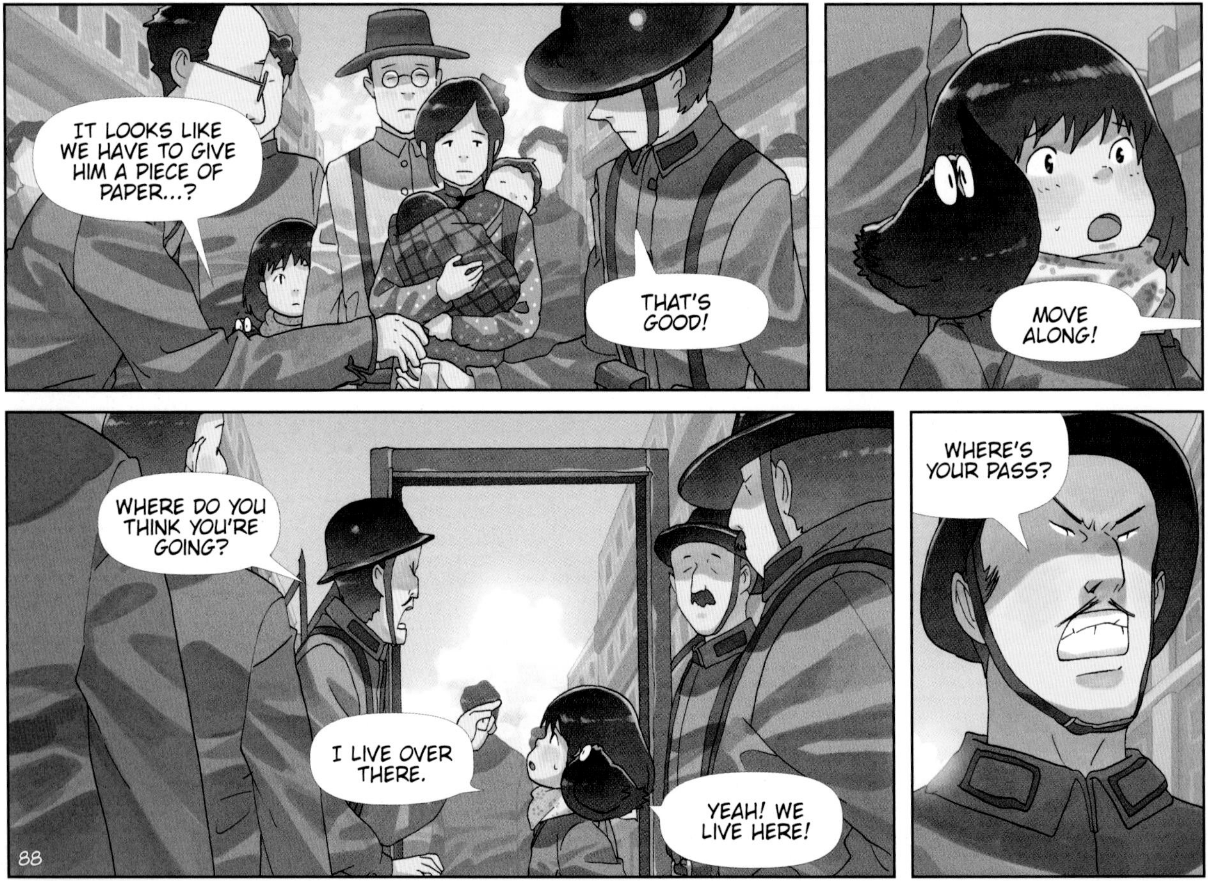
IT LOOKS LIKE WE HAVE TO GIVE HIM A PIECE OF PAPER...?
THAT'S GOOD!
MOVE ALONG!
WHERE DO YOU THINK YOU'RE GOING?
I LIVE OVER THERE.
YEAH! WE LIVE HERE!
WHERE'S YOUR PASS?

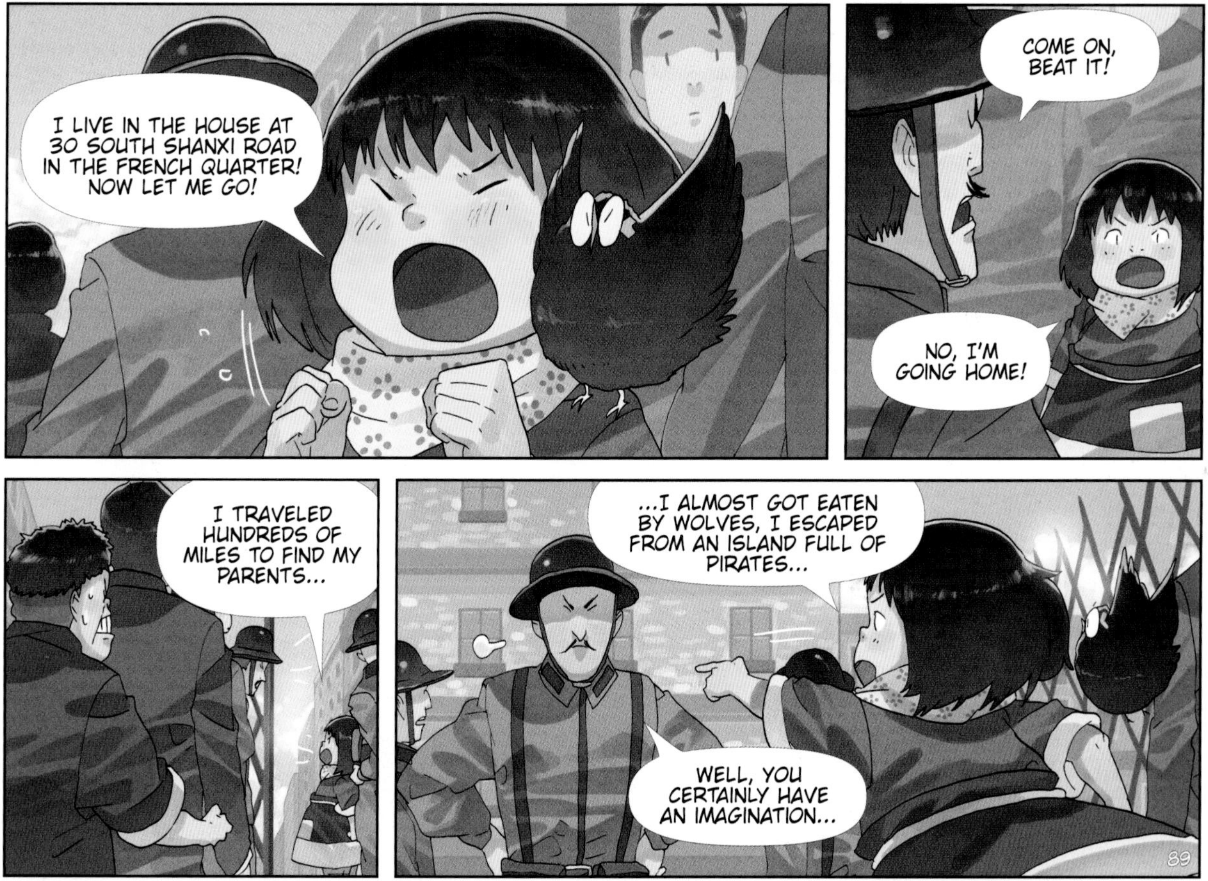
I LIVE IN THE HOUSE AT 30 SOUTH SHANXI ROAD IN THE FRENCH QUARTER! NOW LET ME GO!
COME ON, BEAT IT!
NO, I'M GOING HOME!
I TRAVELED HUNDREDS OF MILES TO FIND MY PARENTS...
...I ALMOST GOT EATEN BY WOLVES, I ESCAPED FROM AN ISLAND FULL OF PIRATES...
WELL, YOU CERTAINLY HAVE AN IMAGINATION...

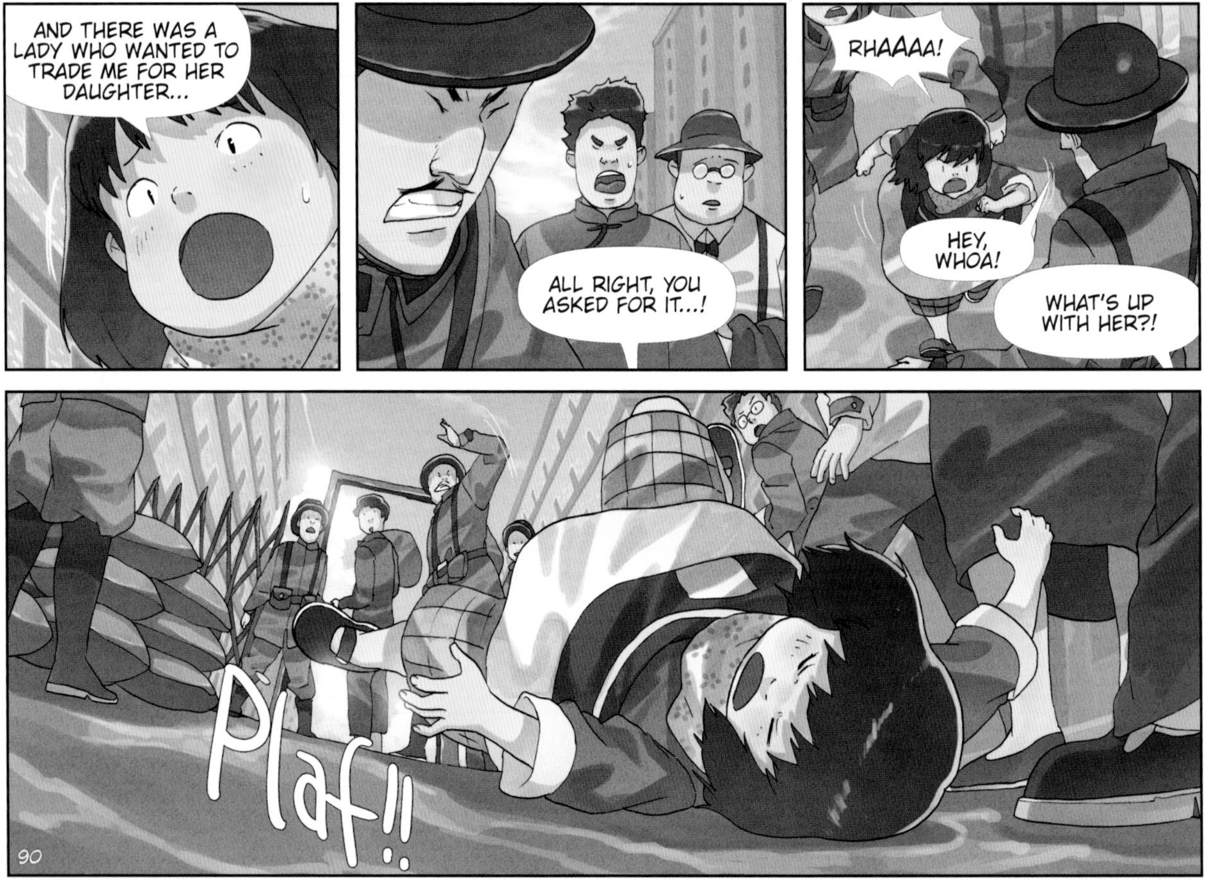
AND THERE WAS A LADY WHO WANTED TO TRADE ME FOR HER DAUGHTER...
ALL RIGHT, YOU ASKED FOR IT...!
RHAAAA!
HEY, WHOA!
WHAT'S UP WITH HER?!
Plaf!!

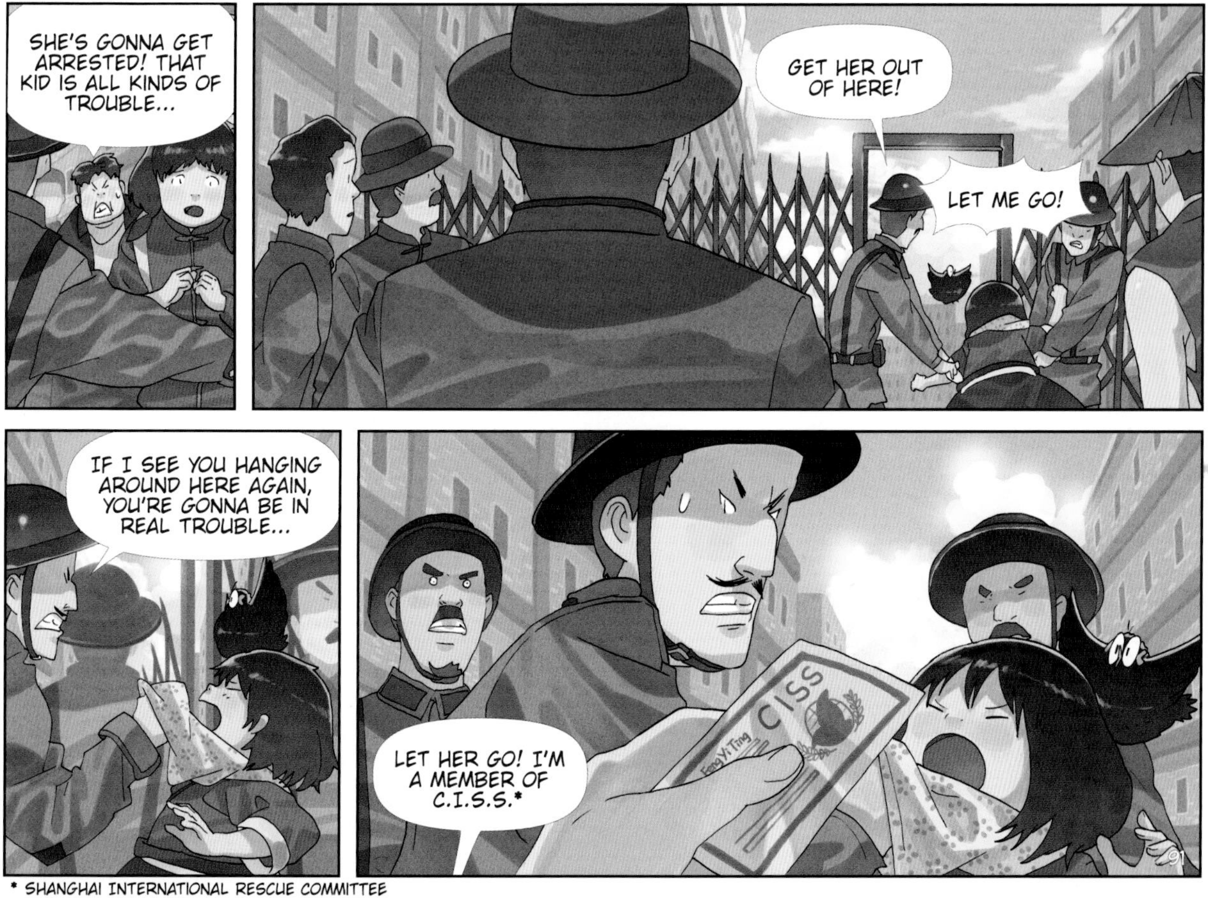
SHE'S GONNA GET ARRESTED! THAT KID IS ALL KINDS OF TROUBLE...
GET HER OUT OF HERE!
LET ME GO!
IF I SEE YOU HANGING AROUND HERE AGAIN, YOU'RE GONNA BE IN REAL TROUBLE...
CISS
Fang Yi Ting
LET HER GO! I'M A MEMBER OF C.I.S.S.*

* SHANGHAI INTERNATIONAL RESCUE COMMITTEE

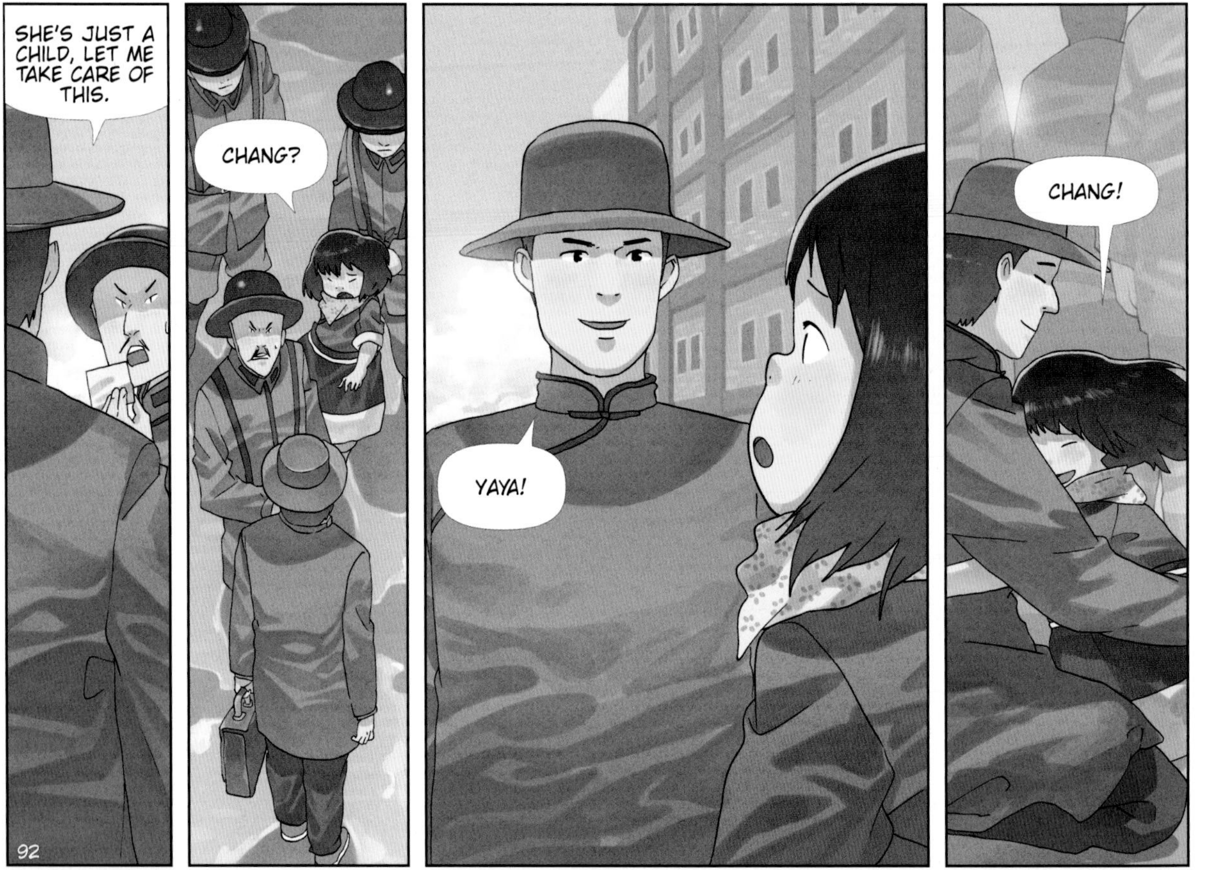
SHE'S JUST A CHILD, LET ME TAKE CARE OF THIS.
CHANG?
YAYA!
CHANG!

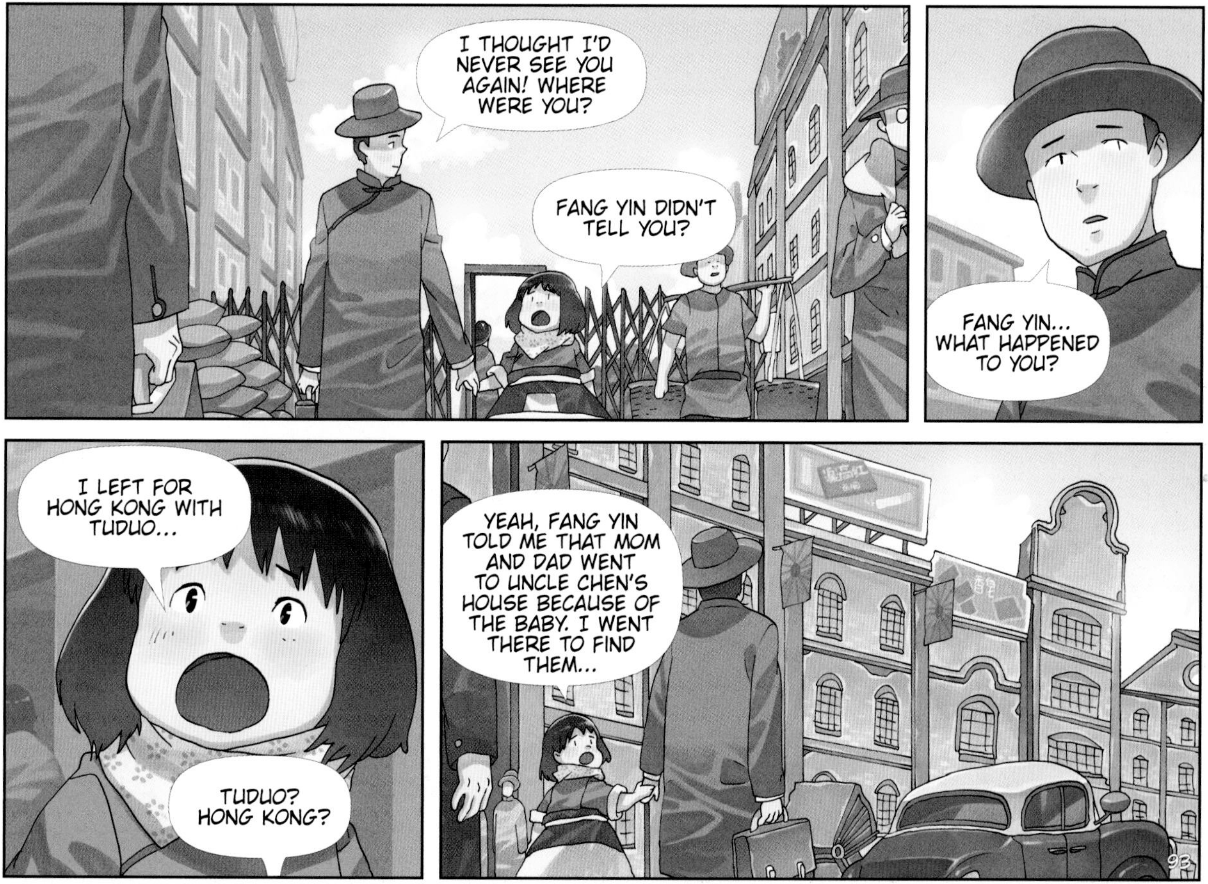
I THOUGHT I'D NEVER SEE YOU AGAIN! WHERE WERE YOU?
FANG YIN DIDN'T TELL YOU?
FANG YIN... WHAT HAPPENED TO YOU?
I LEFT FOR HONG KONG WITH TUDUO...
TUDUO? HONG KONG?
YEAH, FANG YIN TOLD ME THAT MOM AND DAD WENT TO UNCLE CHEN'S HOUSE BECAUSE OF THE BABY. I WENT THERE TO FIND THEM...

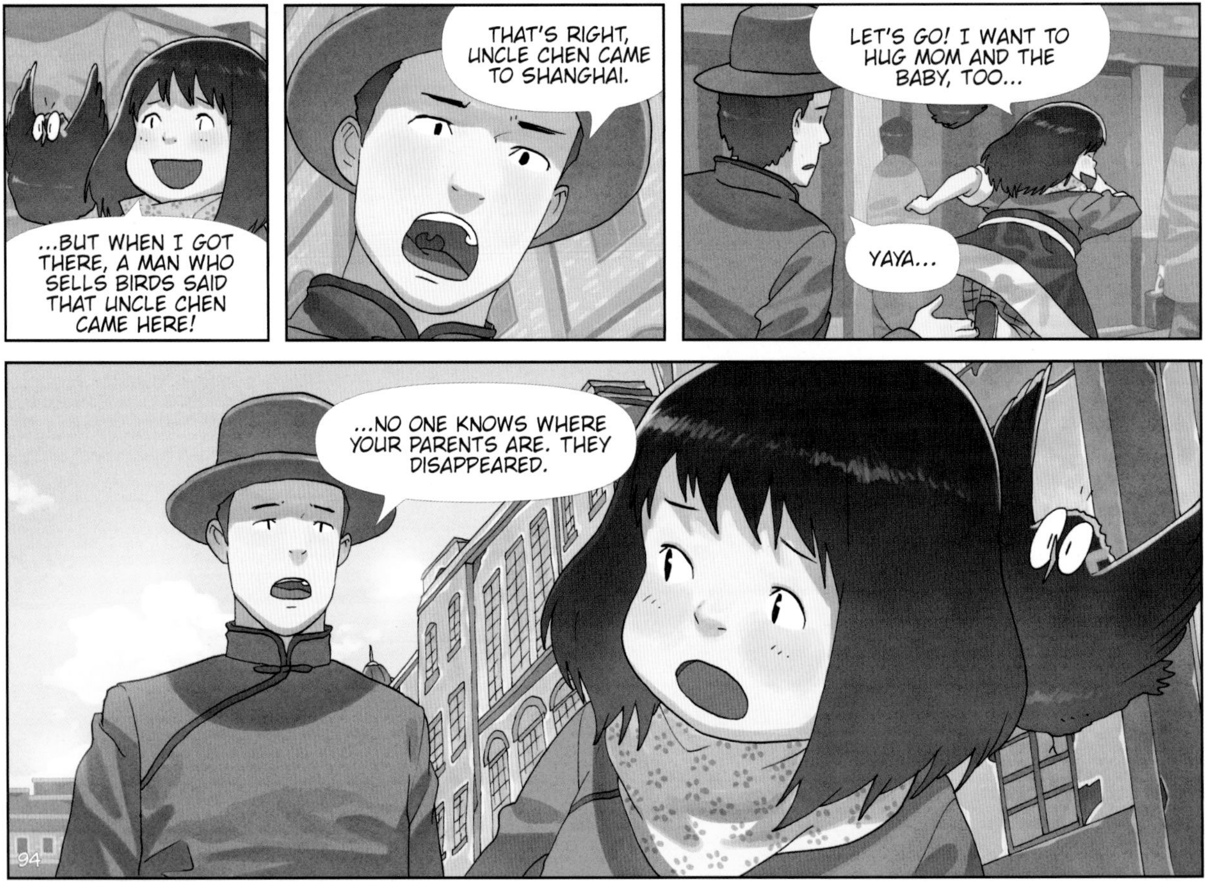
...BUT WHEN I GOT THERE, A MAN WHO SELLS BIRDS SAID THAT UNCLE CHEN CAME HERE!
THAT'S RIGHT, UNCLE CHEN CAME TO SHANGHAI.
LET'S GO! I WANT TO HUG MOM AND THE BABY, TOO...
YAYA...
...NO ONE KNOWS WHERE YOUR PARENTS ARE. THEY DISAPPEARED.

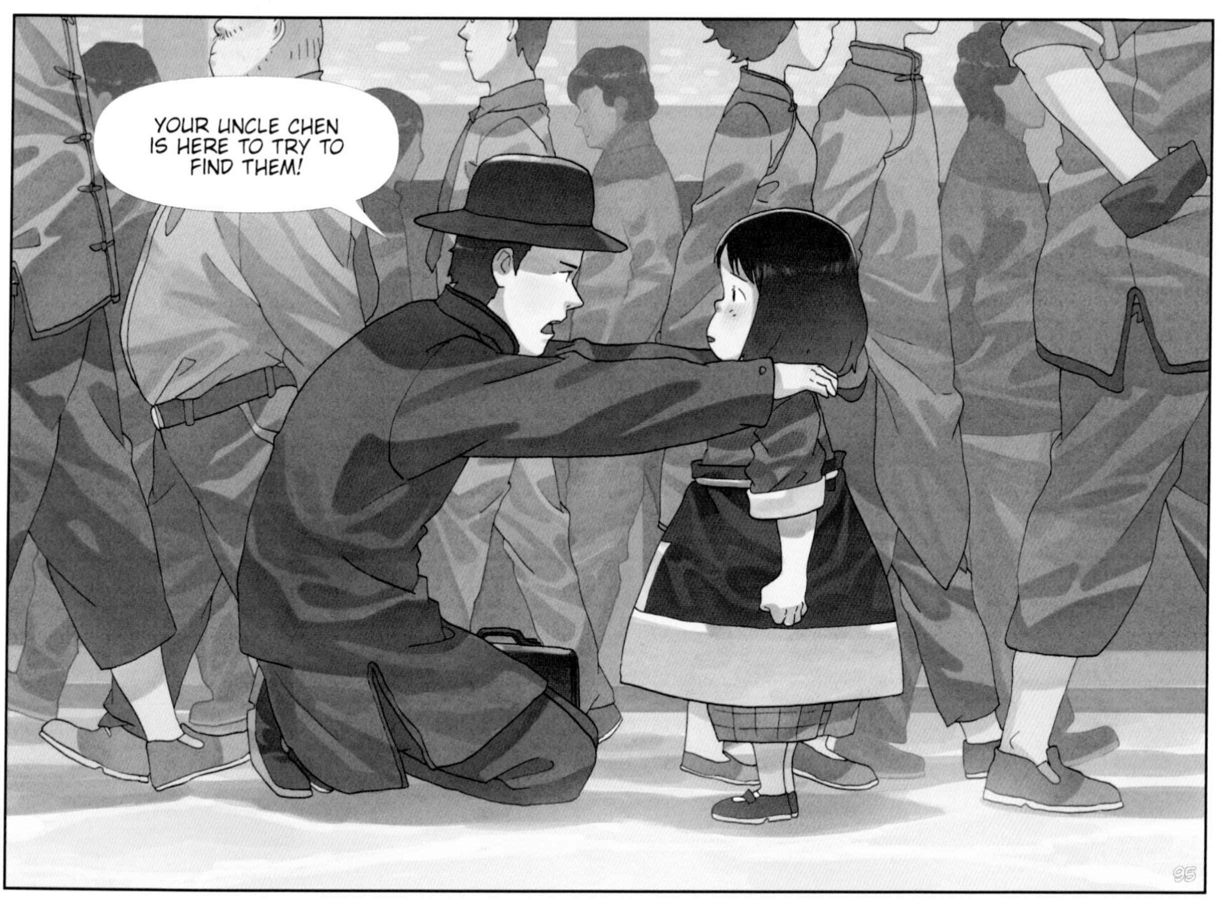
YOUR UNCLE CHEN IS HERE TO TRY TO FIND THEM!

I FINALLY FOUND YAYA AND WE'RE BACK IN SHANGHAI, RID OF THAT MEAN, FAT OAF! BUT WHERE ARE YAYA'S PARENTS?

ISBN: 978-1-951719-01-2
Library of Congress Control Number: 2020915850

The Ballad of Yaya, Vol. 8: The Return, published 2020 by Magnetic Press, LLC.
Originally published in French under the title *La Balade de Yaya 8, Le retour* © Editions Fei 2013/Golo/Omont/Marty/Girard, in partnership with Beijing Total Vision Culture Spreads Co. Ltd. All rights reserved. MAGNETIC PRESS™, and all associated distinctive designs are trademarks of Magnetic Press, LLC. No similarity between any of the names, characters, persons, or institutions in this book with those of any living or dead person or institution is intended, and any such similarity which may exist is purely coincidental.

LES ÉDITIONS FEI

Printed in China.

10 9 8 7 6 5 4 3 2 1